The Chemy Called Al

A NOVEL BY WENDY ISDELL

EDITED BY PAMELA ESPELAND

Free Spirit PUBLISHING

Library of Congress Cataloging-in-Publication Data
Isdell, Wendy, 1975–
The chemy called Al : a novel / by Wendy Isdell ; edited by Pamela Espeland.
    p.   cm.

Sequel to "A gebra named al."
Summary: When her reading light goes out, Julie places her chemistry book under her head, passes through a mysterious portal, and finds herself in the land of Science.

ISBN 0-915793-96-2 (pbk.: alk. paper)

1. Youths' writings, American. [1. Fantasy. 2. Chemistry-Fiction. 3. Youths' writings.]   I. Espeland, Pamela, 1951–   II. Title.
PZ7.I772Ch   1996
[Fic]—dc20   95-32717

    CIP
    AC

Cover and book design by MacLean & Tuminelly
Cover and interior illustrations by Virginia Kylberg

10 9 8 7 6 5 4 3 2 1
Printed in the United States of America

Free Spirit Publishing Inc.
400 First Avenue North, Suite 616
Minneapolis, MN 55401-1730
(612) 338-2068

Acknowledgments

I would like to thank the following persons
for their insightful advice:

Pamela Espeland
Stuart Zolty
Dr. James Grimmer, math teacher
Joseph Michel, science teacher
Ann Miller, language arts teacher
Daniel Naslund, English teacher

Contents

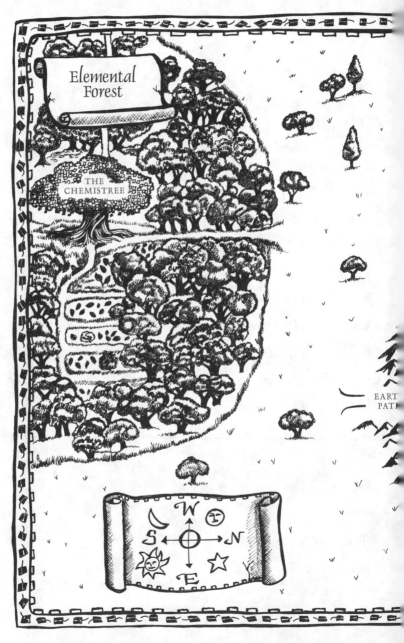

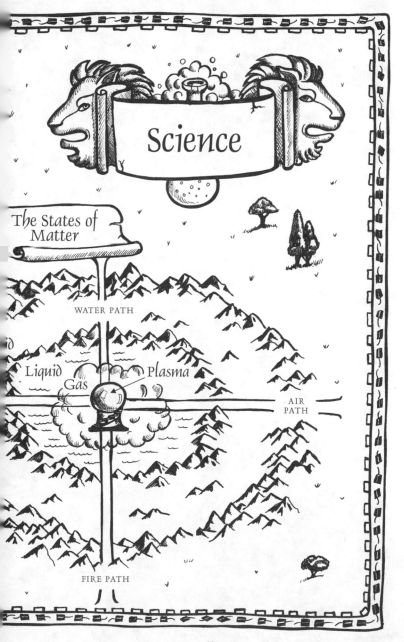

Science

The States of Matter

WATER PATH

Liquid
Gas
Plasma

AIR PATH

FIRE PATH

Who's Who in The Chemy Called Al

In the land of Science, where this story takes place, reside many intelligent creatures who look like horses. They represent the elements of the Periodic Table and their isotopes, so they are called Periodics and Isotopes. The "former Periodics" represent those elements whose names have changed over time. For example, the element we call "gold" used to be called "aurum." If you look for the element gold on the Periodic Table, you'll find it under the symbol "Au" — for Aurum.

In alphabetical order:

Al the Chemy-lion: A lion representing alchemy; his official name is Albertus Leo Magnus, or "Al the Great Cat."

Al the gebra: A zebra representing algebra; Julie's first friend in the land of Mathematics; his "stripes" are actually long lines of equations.

Argentum: A female former Periodic (Silver is the modern equivalent); her color is silver, and her chemical symbol is "Ag."

Astatine: A female Periodic, one of the Halogens; her color is light gray, and her chemical symbol is "At."

Aurum: A male former Periodic (Gold is the modern equivalent); his color is metallic gold, and his chemical symbol is "Au."

Bromine: A male Periodic, one of the Halogens; his color is auburn, and his chemical symbol is "Br."

Chlorine: A female Periodic, one of the Halogens; her color is bright yellow-green, and her chemical symbol is "Cl."

Chromium: A male Periodic; his color is metallic gray, and his chemical symbol is "Cr."

Cuprum: A male former Periodic (Copper is the modern equivalent); his color is metallic orange, and his chemical symbol is "Cu."

Deuterium: A male Isotope, Hydrogen's brother, and a friend of Julie's from *A Gebra Named Al*; his color is silver-gray, and his chemical symbol is "$_1^2$H."

Ferrum: A male former Periodic (Iron is the modern equivalent); his color is dark gray, and his chemical symbol is "Fe."

Fluorine: A female Periodic, one of the Halogens; her color is pale yellow, and her chemical symbol is "F."

Hydrargyrum: A female former Periodic (Mercury is the modern equivalent); her color is dull gray (except in the sun), and her chemical symbol is "Hg."

Hydrogen: A female Periodic, and a friend of Julie's from *A Gebra Named Al*; her color is silver-gray, and her chemical symbol is "H."

Iodine: A male Periodic, one of the Halogens; his color is dark gray, and his chemical symbol is "I."

Julie: A young human female.

Kalium: A female former Periodic (Potassium is the modern equivalent), and a friend of Julie's from *A Gebra Named Al*; her color is silver-white, and her chemical symbol is "K" (like Potassium's).

The Mathematician: The ruler of the land of Mathematics; a tiny, kind-hearted, white-bearded man who wears a blue robe and a simple crown.

Natrium: A female former Periodic (Sodium is the modern equivalent); her color is light gray, and her chemical symbol is "Na."

Plumbum: A male former Periodic (Lead is the modern equivalent); his color is dark gray, and his chemical symbol is "Pb."

Protium: A male Isotope, Hydrogen's brother; his color is silver-gray, and his chemical symbol is "$_1^1H$."

Sodium: A male Periodic, and a friend of Julie's from *A Gebra Named Al*; his color is silver-gray, and his chemical symbol is "Na."

Stannum: A male former Periodic (Tin is the modern equivalent); his color is light gray, and his chemical symbol is "Sn."

Stibnum: A female former Periodic (Antimony is the modern equivalent); her color is silver-white, and her chemical symbol is "Sb."

Tritium: A male Isotope, Hydrogen's brother, and a friend of Julie's from *A Gebra Named Al*; his color is silver-gray, and his chemical symbol is "$_1^3H$."

Tungsten: A male Periodic; his color is light metallic gray with white speckles, and his chemical symbol is "W."

Wendelium: A male Periodic, formerly named Eka-silicon, then renamed with Julie's help; his color is unknown, since he takes the shape of a huge cloud, and his chemical symbol is "Wd."

Wolfram: A male former Periodic (Tungsten is the modern equivalent); his color is light metallic gray, and his chemical symbol is "W."

wolframs: Dangerous servants of the periodic Wolfram; sometimes a wolfram looks like a shaggy brown wolf, at other times like a large, powerful ram.

Author's Preface

The Chemy Called Al is a sequel to *A Gebra Named Al,* but you don't have to read *Gebra* to understand *Chemy.* The two books tell different stories. They share some of the same characters, and there are references in *Chemy* to events that happened in *Gebra,* but each book is complete in itself.

If you haven't read *Gebra* and you're curious about what happens in that book, here's a brief summary:

Late one afternoon, while working on her homework, Julie keeps getting the wrong answer to what looks like a simple algebra problem. Frustrated, she gives up, rests her head on her book, falls asleep, and is awakened by an Imaginary Number who suddenly appears in her room. When she follows the Number through a mysterious portal that opens in the air, she finds herself in the Land of Mathematics. The first creature she meets is a zebra (who's really a *gebra* — pronounced "JEE-bra") named Al.

Al and his friends — scientific "horses" representing elements and their isotopes — agree to take Julie to the Mathematician's Castle for help finding her way back home. Their journey takes them through the Orders of Operations (real places in Mathematics), an attack by the wolframs (servants of the evil Tungsten), and finally to the Mathematician....

A Gebra Named Al takes place in Mathematics; *The Chemy Called Al* is set in the land of Science, which is adjacent to Mathematics. In *Gebra*, Al the gebra represents algebra; in this book, Al the Chemy-lion represents alchemy.

If all you want to do is read the story of *The Chemy Called Al*, you can skip now to Chapter 1, because the rest of this preface has nothing to do with the story itself. Instead, its purpose is to explain the scientific side of alchemy — to note, in particular, how alchemy is the direct ancestor of modern chemistry.

No one seems able to agree where alchemy started. In fact, no one can even say definitively where the word comes from. The two main suggestions are the Greek *chymia*, meaning "the art of melting and alloying metals," and the Arabic *Al Khemia*, with *Khem* being the word for "Egypt" in Arabic. These two languages reflect locations from which alchemy is said to have arisen, although arguments continue to this day as to which is the true birthplace.

Some say the ancient Greeks, particularly Aristotle, provided the seed from which alchemy grew, with its four "States of Matter" (Earth, Air, Fire, and Water). Others say that the ancient Egyptians, with their skills in metallurgy, put forth the first ideas that led to alchemy. Still other sources point to the Chinese and their use of gold as a healing agent millennia before the rise of Western civilization. In fact, the ideas for which alchemy is famous probably came from all of these sources, as well as a heaping helping of Middle Ages superstition and the ever-present, obsessive search for (yes, you guessed it) money.

Whatever the case, alchemy would have surely died of the Dark Ages had not the Arabs, in their widespread conquering, brought all kinds of works — including ones on alchemy — from Alexandria in Egypt and other sites, and translated them all into Arabic. Following the Dark Ages, in about 1100 A.D., scholars then translated these Arabic works into Latin — and the West had, for the first time, a taste of alchemy.

The West apparently liked this taste; alchemy blossomed, splitting shortly thereafter into two branches, the *exoterics* and the *esoterics*.

The esoterics did a lot of thinking. They devised great philosophical dissertations on the "perfect metal" (gold) and how it was formed in the Earth, and how humankind might speed up that process and thus produce gold — and attain spiritual perfection — by making a "Philosopher's Stone" that might transform any base metal into the perfect one. This served to convince later scholars that the alchemists of this period were all nuts who sought fantastical dreams and made up crazy symbolism to convey these ideas. (Coincidentally, the last part is true; alchemical works of this period are so laden with symbolism and imagery as to be incomprehensible to the layperson. Then again, that was the whole idea.)

Because the early alchemists were seeking spiritual perfection, some groups of people (Church-related and secular, modern and historical) have accused them of starting their own occult religion. Others have argued that alchemy was nothing more than a philosophy, unrelated to religion, or else it was a way of seeking Heaven and thus an extension of the religions already in place at that time. I have no answer to this argument. I hold that almost any interpretation may be made of almost any work; you can line up facts and excerpts to prove just about anything you want (at least for an English paper, anyway. With that in mind, maybe you can prove that this Preface is actually a feeble attempt to discuss alchemy).

We turn now to the other branch of alchemy, the one that inspired this book. It was the exoterics, with their endless experimentation, who gave rise to the popular idea of making gold from base metals. Incidentally, there were a number of fraudulent alchemists who did nothing more than cheap tricks in order to milk funds from credulous patrons, and still others who died poor while trying to make themselves rich. But it was the experimentation — the endless hours in the lab mixing chemicals, developing containers for them, and finding ways to maintain heat levels — that concerns us most. These experiments, motivated by greed as they might have been, are what ultimately enabled humankind to discover new elements, monitor their reactions, and begin to quantify chemical relationships. It was this branch of alchemy that gave rise to modern chemistry.

I will not go into more detail here, but countless chemicals were discovered, equipment created, and reactions understood, all because of alchemical tinkering during the Middle Ages. Without alchemy and the experimentation it involved, chemistry in its modern state might not exist at all. Had not alchemists played around for centuries trying to make themselves rich, everyone would have to take Physics in high school to fulfill their science requirement (think about that for a moment). And without alchemy, you wouldn't be reading this book.

So enjoy, and don't worry about knowing more alchemical history; you can learn it in chemistry class.

Wendy Isdell

1
A Tungsten Malfunction

THE FIRST THING Julie noticed was that her reading light went out. She looked up from her homework, blinking, and reached over to click the switch off, then on again. No response.

Julie yawned, stretching, and looked blearily out over her cluttered room. A little light leaked in from behind the curtains, just enough so she could make out the outlines of the more distinctive debris.

There, on the shelf, was the small gray metal box that contained pure lithium. On instructions from the friend who had given it to her, she had never even tried to open it. "My element, Lithium, is very reactive," the friend had warned her. "It will burn on contact with water, even with the humidity in the air." Julie assumed that the element was immersed in oil inside the box.

There, on her desk on top of the clock, drooped the worn and much-used good luck tassel given to her by Al, the gebra. When Julie first met Al, she thought he was a zebra — until she noticed that the black stripes on his white fur were actually long equations arranged in stripes. (The fact that he could talk didn't encourage the idea, either.)

She smiled in the semi-darkness, thinking of the strange friends she had left behind in the even stranger land of Mathematics. When she had followed the Imaginary Number through the portal that suddenly appeared in her room, she hadn't known that she was beginning a great adventure. She hadn't known that she would meet horses representing the elements of the Periodic Table and their isotopes, or that a kindly Mathematician would help her to find her way back home.

Yawning again, she set aside her chemistry book and got up, grumbling about the sun going to bed too early in the wintertime. She crossed the room, navigating past piles of papers, clothes (clean and dirty), Science Fair projects, and overdue library books. She found the far wall by touch and flicked on the overhead light to aid the failing sun. Nothing happened.

"That's odd," she muttered. "Maybe the power's out." She stepped over her bookbag and peered at the electric clock on the desk. The bright red digital numerals still glared 5:17, then changed to 5:18 as she watched. Julie scratched her head and flicked the light switch a few more times. Still nothing. She went out into the hall and, to her amazement, the lights didn't work there, either.

"Now, this is *really* bizarre," she remarked, going back into her room. How could her clock work but not the lights? Reaching up, she turned on the small black-and-white TV on her shelf. The pale numbers jumped to life above the dial, but the screen did not light. She turned up the volume and heard a female weathercaster's voice: "... 54 degrees with low humidity. A nice day in Washington...." Julie turned the volume down again, deeply troubled. *How strange,* she thought again. *No lights, no TV picture, but the electric clock and the TV sound still work.*

Julie shrugged, finally deciding that the problem must be due to unusual power fluctuations or atmospheric conditions. In the light of the TV numerals, she rifled through her desk drawers until she found a candle and a book of matches. What the sun wouldn't provide, and the electric company — or someone — refused to, she would get herself. She scratched one match along the edge of the box. It took three tries, but finally the match flared up and she was able to light the wick. Then she set the candle on the desk, cleared off some old papers — just in case — and retrieved her chemistry book from the bed where she'd left it. *The lights are bound to come on sooner or later,* she thought, *and I might as well get my homework done while I wait.*

"Forms of Light and the Elements," proclaimed the section heading, and Julie chuckled. She knew more about the elements than almost anyone, having met them in person! She kept reading.

"Sodium vapor street lamps, that give off a characteristic yellow color, produce light by the excitation of their electrons...."

After a while Julie yawned a third time, gazing into the

3

golden flame of the candle. Its projected ring of light fell in a quavering three-inch radius on her book, papers, and hands. Blinking, she got up and went to the window, lifting the curtain just enough to glance outside. The streetlight on the corner sent a wash of light over the darkened houses, reflecting yellow in each empty window. Were no one's lights working? She returned to her desk, scratching her head, and turned up the volume on the TV.

"... Live from Channel Five: Emergency Newsbreak! Two nurses and a patient at Washington Hospital were injured today when the new X-ray machine there malfunctioned, emitting X-rays in all directions." There was a pause. "This just in: X-ray machines around the country are having serious malfunctions. While some machines are not working at all, others are emitting unslowed electrons — known as beta rays — into the surrounding area. The reason for this occurrence is unknown. We turn now to Mary Thompson at Washington Hospital for a report...."

Julie turned the volume down. X-ray machines not working? Unslowed electrons? Did electrons move at anything besides the speed of light? Something tugged at the back of her mind, something about a quality that X-ray machines and light bulbs had in common....

Why was there a tight knot in the bottom of her stomach all of a sudden? She jerked her chemistry book forward and flipped to the index, skimming for "X-ray machines."

The indicated page had a diagram showing an "electron emitter" and a "tungsten target."

4

Her heart gave a loud thump, then seemed to stop. With fingers shaking — in excitement or fear, she wasn't sure — she quickly turned back to the section on "Forms of Light and the Elements." Light bulbs. "Light bulbs employ a tungsten filament suspended in a partial vacuum...." Light bulbs, tungsten. X-ray machines, tungsten.

She jumped out of her chair and ran to the encyclopedias down the hall, turning back halfway there to retrieve the candle. As she hunted for the entry on "cathode-ray tubes" such as those found in televisions, she knew that she had already solved the mystery, or at least part of it. Tungsten was a Periodic — a supernatural, equine representative of the element tungsten — who had been rebelling when she had gone to the land of Mathematics; his servants, the wolframs, had attacked her and her companions. Now the things in her world that used tungsten weren't working....

There was the page she was looking for. "Cathode-ray tubes employ a tungsten filament...."

Julie dropped the encyclopedia and sat there in shock, chewing idly on her lower lip. This meant trouble in a big way. There was a problem with Tungsten again. And there was no way she could return to Mathematics, even if she had known what to do. Had Tungsten taken over? Or perhaps he was dead, and that's why his element wasn't working on Earth. What if her friends — Al, and the Periodics, and the Mathematician — were in danger? She brought the candle back to her room and went to her shelf, taking down the small gray box on which was engraved the figure of a running horse and the chemical symbol "Li." It was preternaturally cool and heavy in her hands. She turned it over, inspecting the seamless corners and the smooth underside. She traced the horse figure's flowing mane, thinking of the silver-white one belonging to her friend, the Periodic Lithium. That, and of the soft fuzz that covered his whole body.

That made her think of Al and his equation-striped white fur. She took down the worn black braid of hair that had come from the tassel of his zebra-like tail.

"Al," she murmured to herself, "it looks like I'll see you again soon." She put down the box, for it was too heavy to lug around, despite its diminutive size, and tied the braid around one belt-loop of her jeans. There had to be *some* way to get back to Mathematics!

She plopped down at her desk, disregarding the candle she had left on the shelf across the room. She had to think. She had been brought to Mathematics the first time through a peculiar set of circumstances. She had fallen asleep on her algebra book, and the Imaginary Number had appeared, looking like a white, translucent cloud. Behind him had been the portal, like an inkblot in the air. It had been an accident the first time, but could she cause the portal to appear again? She had wondered off and on in the past whether she could, but she had never really had a reason to try. Now, knowing that something must be terribly wrong in Mathematics, she knew she must attempt to journey there again.

She fished through her bookbag in the dim light, looking for her Algebra Two book, only to discover that she had left it at school. She sat back down at her desk, her legs shaking up and down rapidly with nervous energy. What should she do? It didn't seem likely that there would be school tomorrow, since all the lights were out, so she couldn't just wait and get her book then. Besides, another day might be too late for Mathematics, if things there were as bad as she suspected.

She looked down at her chemistry book. She knew there was a land adjacent to Mathematics called Science. But would a portal open to that land if she tried sleeping on a science book?

She thought again of the vicious wolframs and how her friends had bravely defended her. The shaggy, fanged beasts had been in wolf form, eerily crying "Human! Human! Human!" Julie shuddered, remembering. They had wanted to capture her because she was a Human, and Humans had power in those lands. She was unsure what those powers might be — she had never really seen any sign of such abilities in herself — but she had seen the instant respect accorded her wherever she went last time.

Her thoughts drifted to the Mathematician, the kindly old man who had finally sent her home. He, and all of her other friends, could be in serious trouble if Tungsten had launched a major revolt. She owed it to them to at least try to help.

Julie looked down at the book again. She had to try.

There's practically no light in the room, so it would be easy to go to sleep, she thought. She dumped everything out of her bookbag and threw in everything within arm's reach that might come in handy: her pocket-knife, a jacket, dried fruit, a bottled soda, and the gold watch her parents had given her for her last birthday. Then she tied on her sneakers, snuffed out the candle, and sprawled out on her bed, clutching the bookbag, with the chemistry book under her head.

She tossed and turned for nearly half an hour, watching the shifting red clock digits methodically tick off the minutes. Gradually her eyelids grew heavy and she felt a surge of vertigo. Then everything went black.

The blackness did not last long. Julie felt herself suspended in space, not falling but not standing on anything either. Colored streaks of light appeared and grew brighter as she watched them. She relaxed, recognizing the portal to Mathematics, and inspected the lights. They were magenta, yellow, and cyan, forming patterns that looked like simple computer graphics she had seen before. They began somewhere behind her — she found she couldn't turn around to see — and ended somewhere far ahead.

Okay, she concluded, *I'm in the portal. Now what?*

As if in response, the lights faded quickly to black, and she thought she lost consciousness again. Then she opened her eyes.

She saw her ceiling. She was back in her room.

Frustrated, she sat up and looked toward her desk — and froze. Hovering in the air between her and her desk, even darker than the darkness of her room, was a black oval about six feet high and four feet wide. She could barely make out the multi-colored streaks of light inside that characterized the portal to Mathematics.

"I did it!" She grabbed her bookbag, slung it over her shoulder, and took a tentative step toward the portal, gazing into its depths. Did she really want to do this?

It's now or never, she thought, and for some reason that old saying seemed more menacing than it ever had before. Taking a quick breath, she took several paces toward the portal and stepped inside. As she passed its black border, there came a burst of the color streaks and another moment of blackness. Then blinding white light bled swiftly in, flooding out the darkness and her vision.

♀ ☾ ♂ ▽ ☿ ⊕

When the radiance faded and Julie could see again, she found herself in a forest glade. Birds chirruped softly high above, and lush vegetation filled the air with a deep, green, earthy smell.

A breeze stirred the stately trees all around her, and dappled spots of light chased each other in circles over the ivy, ferns, and tiny flowers that protruded from the fallen leaves. Julie took a deep breath of the warm air. She had forgotten how pleasant Mathematics could be.

Or perhaps this is Science, thought Julie, *because I used my chemistry book.*

There didn't seem to be a particular path here, but the space beneath the trees was sufficiently open to let her walk easily. Every step left a trail of dark, overturned leaves and that rich scent she enjoyed so much. The leaves were piled so thickly and were so old that they barely rustled, but instead disintegrated beneath her feet. Apparently no one had been here in quite a while.

She kept walking and soon found a long, wide indentation in the forest floor, rather like a flattened rut, that could have been a path or road long ago. She paused at its edge and looked down both leaf-strewn directions. Neither one seemed to lead anywhere definite with any rapidity. So, shrugging, she turned right and followed the loam-blanketed road, continuing for several hours. The dappling slowly shifted from one side of the trees to the other, and she saw no living creatures besides the cheeping birds. After a while, Julie found herself sighing. This place was very peaceful, but she was getting lonesome. Where was everyone?

The path started widening and she saw bright green up ahead, indicating a glade or meadow.

Or maybe even the end of the woods, she thought hopefully. *And outside, there might be people . . . or intelligent animals,* she amended, thinking of her friends, who were not precisely human.

She came to the open space only to discover that it was a rather small meadow surrounded by thick forest on all sides. In the center was the largest, oldest tree she had ever seen. Its trunk was three times her width, bolstered by thick roots that boiled up onto the grass in every direction. Its canopy of leaves threw the entire right three-fourths of the glade into shadow and began where the surrounding trees were tapering off. Julie stood agape for a moment, then moved into the shadow with some trepidation. As she got nearer to the trunk, she saw a small brass plate fastened to it with screws about six feet up. She stood on tiptoe to read it:

The Chemistree
Original Progenitor
of All Modern Species

Julie stepped back a few feet, eyeing the riveted trunk. Was this the original of all those chemistrees she had seen out in the grasslands between here and Upper Mathematics? Her eyes traveled up its length again to the leaves. They appeared to be square, with small, round fruit dangling among the branches.

Square leaves? Julie swished through the tall grass until she found a fallen twig with some leaves still clinging to it, and inspected them. On each corner was inscribed a tiny letter: "E," "A," "F," and "W."

Julie walked around the trunk to the other side, where she was surprised to find a large recess. She stood again on tiptoe to peer inside and saw a giant tome. Pocketing the square leaves, she reached in carefully to get the book, and found that its weight made it extremely difficult to move. Grunting, she braced herself against the trunk and lifted carefully, drawing the book out with infinite care. It seemed to be centuries old and smelled of musty leather and paper. She sat down on the grass with the book in her lap, fingering the worn cover. Its title was illegible, worn away long ago by unknown fingers.

She cautiously opened the ratty cover. The inside was covered with calligraphy in some foreign language Julie didn't know. She scanned the words but was unable to decipher any. Over and over, she saw a word that looked like "atomos." She knew that was the Greek for "atom," meaning "indivisible," and figured that the book could be about the history of science. But why was it inside the Chemistree?

Julie lifted the pages open in sections, noting the concise script and the occasional Roman numeral. She skipped a large section at random and suddenly encountered English:

June 14, 1849. The Implied Permission policy has been formally challenged by the Periodic Emeritus Aurum, who seeks to revoke that policy for the first time. A council of other Periodics Emeriti, after much debate, has voted to reject his proposed denial of Implied Permission on the grounds that there is insufficient cause to do so. Implied Permission, which was first instituted at the height of the Bronze Age in the Human world, is the code that enables Humans to utilize elemental substances without specific permission and/or supervision by the Periodic in question. It was designed to ease the work load of the Periodics and to facilitate scientific development in the Human world. With minor exceptions, it has functioned flawlessly since its commencement.

"What is it you are doing there?"

Julie gasped at the soft, aged-sounding voice, and her head jerked up. She saw a brilliantly glinting, gold-colored being before her. It — or he, by the voice — moved easily into the shade about ten feet away, and his blinding halo faded. He was a Periodic. She recognized the intelligent equine form from her last visit.

She gaped at him for a moment, her eyes lighting on the "Au" emblazoned on his shoulder. Then they traveled to his face. His eyes were deepest gray, and a short beard sprouted from his chin.

"What?" she finally managed to get out.

"I said, 'What is it you are doing there?'" The Periodic shifted his weight ever so slightly.

"I ... I'm just reading," she blurted.

"You can read?" The horse's ears perked forward momentarily, then fell back to rest.

"Yes." Julie set the book in the grass and stood up. "I am Julie, a human." She started to extend her hand for a shake, then let it drop awkwardly.

The Periodic's ears shot forward now and stayed there. He raised his head slightly, taking a whiff of the air.

"Pardon me," he said finally, "but my eyes aren't as good as they used to be. You do *smell* Human."

Julie nodded, still staring at his metallic fur. "Are you Gold?" she inquired, knowing that every element on the Periodic Table had a Periodic to represent it.

The Periodic chuckled. "No, I'm Aurum.... His predecessor," he added at her distressed look.

"Oh," Julie said, nodding. "Like Kalium?" She thought of her female friend, Potassium's predecessor, who had introduced her to the Council of Periodics.

"Yes, very much like Kalium. Do you know her?"

"Yes. I've been here before."

"Ah." Aurum nodded sagely, his thin beard fluttering in the wind. "But surely not *here*." He pointed his nose toward the giant tree.

"No. In Mathematics."

Aurum chuckled again. "You're a long way from Mathematics."

"Where am I?"

"You mean you don't know?" Aurum shot her a steady look from one steel-gray eye. "You're in the center of the Elemental Forest in Science."

"Oh, good!" exclaimed Julie. "That's where I want to be."

"It is?"

"Yes. I'm looking ... I mean, I'm wondering...." She didn't know how much to tell Aurum of the Tungsten-related trouble in her world.

Aurum paced toward her bookbag beside the tree. "I haven't been here a while myself. I wouldn't have come today, but I sensed my element.... If you don't mind...." He dexterously applied his teeth to the fabric strap of her bookbag and flipped the top open with his nose. "Ah, here we are." He lifted his head from within the bag, and her gold watch dangling delicately between his front teeth. "About ten karat, I believe," he muttered around the watch. He brought her the instrument, which she wiped off on her jeans and fastened around her wrist.

"What else do you have in here?" muttered Aurum, returning to her bookbag. Julie scratched her head but didn't say anything. After all, there was nothing private in there. Aurum nosed out the bottle of cola. "Silicon dioxide, solidified hydrocarbon by-product, carbonic acid under pressure, water...."

"You can tell all that by looking at it?" Julie scooped up the bottle and twisted off the cap. Aurum jumped at the hiss.

"You should be careful with that! You just removed the pressure. Look, the carbonic acid is decomposing into carbon dioxide and water."

"Uh, yeah." Julie nodded, taking a short drink from the bottle. "That's why it bubbles."

"You drink it?" Aurum was aghast.

"Of course. Want some?"

"No! Er, no, thank you." Aurum watched her in fascination for a moment, then turned back to her bag.

"Hmm, stainless steel...." Aurum pushed her sheathed pocket-knife toward her. "Very nice. Bessemer process?"

"What? I don't know."

Aurum put her knife back in the bag with his mouth. "The Bessemer process is a method of making steel. It was new...." Aurum drifted off. "I guess it isn't new any longer." He picked up the bag and brought it to her. "Put the book back, please, Human."

Julie took her bookbag, then put it down again, momentarily

flustered. She carefully replaced the ancient book in the tree, then turned in time to see Aurum trotting into the forest.

"Wait!" she cried. She slung her bookbag over one shoulder, grabbed her soda, and hurried to follow him.

"I'm not going far," countered the aged former Periodic. "Argentum! Argentum! I found it!" he called.

"Who?" Julie stopped running, a little short of breath.

"Argentum!" shouted Aurum again, also pausing. "Hey, Ag! I found that gold!"

Julie took another short drink of cola, then replaced the cap and slipped the bottle into her bag. She heard leaves rubbing together to one side, and when her head followed the sound, there stood another horse.

"Aurum, stop," it reproved in a matronly tone. "You're disturbing the whole forest."

"Oh, there you are, Ag," sighed Aurum, trotting toward her and nuzzling her. "Look what I found."

"Yes, I see. A Human." The new horse stepped onto the path, and her light gray fur blazed into white light. Julie squinted, holding up one hand.

"Are you Argentum?" she queried. "You look like Silver."

"Yes." Argentum stepped into the shade on the other side of the path and stood gazing at her. "Silver is my modern name, in the Human world. He holds my office now."

Julie nodded, glancing at Aurum. "Like Kalium has been replaced by Potassium."

"Yes."

Aurum trotted back toward Julie and stuck his nose into her bag. "She had a gold watch in here.... Wait, she's wearing it."

"Oh?" Argentum pointed her ears at him, then swished her tail. "What are you going to do with her?"

"Do with her?" he repeated, his nose still in Julie's bookbag.

"Yes, *do* with her. Is she a new pet?" The female Periodic chuckled, followed by Aurum.

Julie knew better than to look at him when he was standing in the sun — as he was now, poking through her bag — but she did anyway and was blinded. "I'm not a pet," she insisted, shielding her eyes with one hand.

"No, we know you're not," Argentum explained. "It was always Wolfram that had those nasty pets."

"The wolframs?" Julie gasped. "Big, mean, shaggy wolves with glowing eyes?"

"Yes, that sounds about right," Argentum asserted. "I take it you've had problems with them."

"The last time I was here, they attacked me on the way to the Mathematician, while I was trying to get home. Do you have problems with them, too?"

"Oh, yes. They used to dig in my silver mine and my garden. Horrible beasts."

"Used to?" Julie followed Argentum as the silvery horse started back toward the Chemistree.

"Not anymore," explained Argentum. "They left when Wolfram did."

"Who is Wolfram?" Julie realized that this was the second mention of that name. "Is he the leader of the wolframs?"

"In a way," stated Argentum.

"But he's not a wolfram himself," Aurum clarified. "He's Tungsten's predecessor."

"Tungsten? The crazy Periodic who's trying to take over Mathematics?"

Both former Periodics stopped but did not turn around.

"Did you say Tungsten was plotting, or Wolfram?" Argentum swiveled her ear to catch Julie's reply.

"Well, the last time I was here, everyone said it was Tungsten."

They turned around then, their mouths set grimly. "Tungsten is probably not behind the mischief," stated Argentum. "But Wolfram has been missing for quite a while, and he always had delusions of grandeur."

"He's been hit in the head with a few too many electrons, if you ask me," put in Aurum.

Julie laughed out loud, thinking of the X-ray machines that had stopped working in her world. They used a piece of tungsten to slow down super-fast electrons and produce X-rays.

"Julie," Aurum said, "why don't you wait here for a little while? We are going to get the others." With that, the two horses broke into a trot and disappeared into the forest. Julie was alone again.

2

A Growl in the Forest

JULIE SIGHED, scuffing the grass with her sneaker. She assumed that "the others" meant the other former Periodics, including her friend Kalium. But how long would it take for Aurum and Argentum to find them and bring them here?

She wandered back into the quiet woods, away from the direction her new friends had gone. As before, there was no path, but the leaf-cushioned area beneath the trees was sufficiently open to let her walk freely. She did not walk far, mindful of her returning companions, but the heavy silence and solemn columns of tree trunks made her feel a thousand miles away from any living being.

As she passed by a thick cluster of spiky bushes, she heard a low, savage growl behind her. Gasping, she swiveled and found herself staring into the stark yellow eyes of a scruffy, snarling canine animal.

It growled again, louder, and crouched low to the ground. Its mouth gaped open and issued a fierce snarl.

"Human!"

Julie jumped, then shrieked, recognizing the beast as a wolfram. Nearly paralyzed by terror, she leaped away from it, stumbled, and ran as hard as she could.

The animal gave chase, howling, "Human! Human! Human!" at her heels. Julie fled, gasping for breath, tripping in the piled foliage and running into branches that clawed at her face. The wolfram snapped at her heels, tripping her again, and she kicked desperately backwards at it, missing, crawling forward.

"Human! Human! Hu —" The beast's terrible cry was drowned out by a ferocious roar from directly above. Julie, trying to climb up from her knees, slipped yet again on the wet leaves and lay there, breathing hard, her mind blank, face down.

She heard the wolfram retreat, yelping in terror. After a moment, she rolled over, staring up into the foliage but seeing nothing. Her weary mind refused to function.

"Human," she sighed softly, wondering where the roar had come from and what had scared away the wolfram. She sat up trembling, catching her breath.

Something large rustled in the branches above, but she still saw nothing.

"Hello?" she called. "Who is it?" Her breathing was nearly

back to normal now. "Whoever you are, thanks for scaring that wolfram off."

"Gratitude is acknowledged." The deep voice rippled from directly above her. Julie stood and peered into the trees, more curious than afraid. After all, this creature – or thing – had saved her. Slowly, concentrating, she thought she could make out the outline of several details. A massive paw, a tuft of hair, a large, almond-shaped eye....

"Who *are* you?" Julie strained her eyes, but the thing above her shifted – its details dissolving into new, vaguely seen shapes.

"One is Chemy as you are Human," the creature above her purred deeply.

"A Chemy?" Julie queried, still gazing at him. The word sounded like "kemmie."

"Yes. More precisely" – the creature leaped down, shifting colors in midair, blurring, then resolving into a four-legged, chest-high beast with fur and claws – "a Chemy-lion."

Julie gaped as he paced in front of a dark brown tree trunk, the segment of him in front of the tree shifting to exactly match that color. The rest of him remained a nondescript brown-green that merged perfectly with the forest floor. His long, lithe tail twitched as he sniffed the ground where the wolfram had been. What on Earth was a Chemy-lion?

"You wander far," the Chemy-lion interrupted her thoughts.

"Um, yes," Julie agreed, wondering exactly how he meant that. "Can you take me back to the Chemistree?"

The beast, his almond-shaped eyes glimmering with a faint

green tinge, gazed at her and announced, "Chemistree, the foundation and center of the Elemental Forest — one has always led the way there." The Chemy twitched his tail, looking proud, so Julie assumed he was talking about himself.

Julie was about to ask the Chemy-lion what he meant when suddenly he turned and paced through the overturned leaves. Julie followed, staring at his rippling fur. He passed a bright green fern, and a green patch slid across his brownish fur as he walked on.

"Are you transparent?" inquired Julie.

The Chemy-lion twitched an ear, still padding back toward the clearing. "Reflecting one's environment is not the same as revealing it."

"Does that mean you're not transparent?"

The lion's ear twitched again. "The mockingbird mimics sounds it hears. The Chemy-lion mimics colors."

"So you change your own color to match what's around you?"

The lion nodded.

"What color are you really?"

The lion shook his mane, as if throwing off water, but did not reply. Frustrated, Julie followed him silently back to the Chemistree clearing, where the great beast sat back on his haunches, gazing up at the massive tree.

"Aurum told me to wait here until he came back," Julie explained.

The lion rumbled. "The sun moves in sequences of hours. Waiting makes empty time."

Julie shook her head, unable to understand, and watched as the Chemy-lion phased into different shades of green, sniffing the grass around the tree.

"One must seek out the sun in order to get what one seeks," continued the Chemy-lion ambiguously. He looked at her, twitched his tail, and set off in the direction that Aurum and Argentum had taken, nose to the ground. Julie hastened to follow and found a narrow path. The Chemy-lion was graying, browning, and greening farther down. As she hurried after him, Julie looked downward. There were huge, black, five-toed paw prints on the ground.

"You're leaving tracks," she called.

"One must leave clues to allow Humans to follow." The Chemy-lion had disappeared around a bend with his long stride, but his deep voice projected easily back to her.

After a while, the dark prints began to contain brilliant white specks that cast a pale light over the shadowed walkway. The prints looked a little like a star-strewn night sky. Julie stared at them in wonder. The path branched, then branched again. Julie was so fascinated by the prints that she nearly bumped into their creator. He had stopped on the path and was gazing out at a little clearing. On the far side, at the edge of the woods, Aurum was picking something out of the ground with his teeth. The lion watched, saying nothing, then paced forward again. Julie saw that his brilliant paw prints were now multi-hued, like a rainbow swirled together and poured into indentations in the ground.

"Wow," she breathed as they approached Aurum. The grass distorted the effect, but she could still make out the brilliant colors.

"Hey, Aurum, what are you doing?" she called, then noticed that he was chewing vigorously on something.

Aurum lifted his head, gazing blankly at them, then smiled. As she got closer, Julie saw a long, vine-like root hanging out of his mouth.

"Eating," replied the former Periodic.

"Eating what?"

"Golden seal."

Julie eyed the green-and-brown root. It didn't look golden. But if Aurum thought so.... Just then Argentum entered the clearing, followed by three other horses. One was dark gray, one was light gray, and the other was a shimmering metallic orange.

"Aurum! Where are the others?" Argentum admonished him. Then she saw the Chemy-lion. She blinked, then put one fore-leg forward, bent the other, and ducked her head in a formal equine bow.

"Greetings, Albertus Leo Magnus," she stated solemnly.

Aurum suddenly seemed to notice the Chemy-lion. "Hey, Al the Great Cat!" he exclaimed, and Julie realized that the name he had called the Chemy-lion was a modernized version of the name Argentum had used.

"Your name is Al?" she asked the Chemy-lion, nearly giggling at the coincidence. On both trips to this world, she had met an Al!

"The Chemy-lion," purred the beast firmly.

"Al Chemy-lion," repeated Julie softly. "Al Chemy. Alchemy. The art of changing base metals to gold?" She glanced at Aurum, who was offering Al Chemy-lion some golden seal. "I thought that was just superstition."

"Alchemy is the search for perfection, whether spiritual, physical, or chemical," asserted Al, turning away from Aurum. "Different Humans have different views."

"... Although I *was* a major issue," noted Aurum, continuing his snack. "With all that transformation silliness."

"So does that mean you can turn lead into gold?" Julie inquired of the Chemy-lion. At her words, the dark gray newcomer suddenly scowled at her, as did Aurum.

"Why must it always be lead?" the dark horse complained.

"And why gold?" Aurum echoed.

The Chemy-lion chuckled. "An abundant element and a precious one."

The two horses were not mollified.

"Julie, in the Human world, gold was considered the perfect metal," Argentum explained. "In medieval times, that is, and somewhat before. So alchemy, the art of achieving perfection, naturally aimed to produce the perfect metal."

"Why doesn't anyone remember the Philosopher's Stone?" the dark horse grumbled. "Why always transmutation?"

"What stone?" Julie queried.

"The Philosopher's Stone," Argentum explained, "which, the legends say, had great healing powers."

"Legends?" the Chemy-lion rumbled. Argentum shot him a cautious look from the corner of her eye.

"Well," Argentum said abruptly, "the Human alchemist Albertus Magnus sought the Philosopher's Stone, but I don't believe he ever found it."

"Albertus Magnus? But isn't that *your* name?" Julie asked the Chemy-lion.

The great beast nodded.

"The Human must have been named after the Chemy-lion," Aurum put in. "Or else it was just a coincidence."

"Were you his teacher, Al Chemy-lion?"

The Chemy-lion made a soft growl deep in his throat, not answering, then paced closer to her. "You are not Julie Small Human Female," he stated. "I am not Al Chemy-lion."

"Just Al, then?" Julie inquired.

"Just Chemy."

"You prefer 'Chemy' to 'Albertus'?"

"'Chemy' is one of my names, as 'Human' is one of yours."

Julie scratched her head, thinking that the Chemy-lion was confusing species with given names. But then she changed her mind, noticing how she was already thinking of him as "Al Chemy-lion," just as the Periodics considered her "Julie Human." One's species did become part of one's name, under these circumstances.

"Well," began Argentum, as if changing the subject, "let's find the others."

"The other what?" Julie asked.

"The other former Periodics," answered the metallic orange Periodic, turning to peer into the woods behind them.

"Oh!" Argentum exclaimed, pointing her nose at the three other horses. "Julie, this is Natrium, Cuprum, and Plumbum." The light gray, orange, and dark gray horses nodded in order as they were named, the orange one turning again to face her.

Julie gazed at the new horses. The light gray one was extremely soft-looking and larger than all the others. Natrium looked feminine to Julie, but she couldn't be sure. Cuprum, the metallic orange one, was smaller and seemed masculine. He stood out front in the group, gazing boldly around. The last, Plumbum, was obviously the predecessor of Lead, from his remarks if not his charcoal color and great mass. He was heavier than everyone and physically larger than Aurum, Argentum, and Cuprum, Julie noted.

Argentum strode out of the clearing, the others close behind. Al Chemy flicked one ear. "We have followed the sun and now shall follow the moon," he commented. Julie shrugged and trailed after him. This time, to her disappointment, there were no bright footprints to watch.

They walked in a mass down a wide, clear, but extremely convoluted path for some distance. Soon they came to a side path on the left and took that. They walked for quite a while, and Julie was beginning to get footsore when they came to an iron signpost jutting up among the trees to the left that announced "Fe" in ancient script. There was a narrow path beside it, which they followed. Almost immediately, an intricate iron fence sprang up on either side. It increased in height as they continued until it was over ten feet tall.

"Where are we going?" Julie queried.

"This is where Ferrum lives," replied Cuprum, several paces ahead of her.

They reached an immense iron gridwork gate at the end of the fence corridor and had to stop. Julie admired it while Argentum used her teeth to pull a small iron chain that hung from the top. A deep bell pealed three times, and a massive, dark gray, ancient-looking horse stepped out of the growth behind the gate. He somberly returned their gazes for a moment, then nodded at the gate, and it swung open.

"Greetings, Ferrum," Argentum hailed him as the group entered. "We have a matter of some importance, and we need to call a Council."

Ferrum did not reply or even move. He was actually smaller than the rest of the group, but to Julie he still seemed large. There was just something about him.

"If you could meet us out by the Chemistree in an hour," continued Argentum, "it would be much appreciated."

Ferrum's eyes flicked toward Julie, and he stirred at last. "A Human," his deep voice rumbled. He gazed at her, and Julie became uncomfortably aware of knowledge and experience that was vastly greater than her own. It was a sensation that had been growing for a while, but the others' personalities had distracted her from that uneasy observation. Now she perceived it — and it was increasingly disconcerting. Julie fidgeted with her hair.

"She has come about a problem in her world," Argentum put in as the unofficial spokesperson — or spokeshorse — for the group.

Ferrum nodded once. "I will be there."

Without further discussion, Argentum led the group out. When they got back to the main path, Argentum turned to Natrium. "Do you think you could get Kalium to come to the meeting?"

Natrium nodded, shot a curious glance at Julie, and cantered down the path in the direction from which they had come.

Next, Argentum turned to Aurum. "Since it was your job anyway —"

"Hey!" protested Aurum.

"— why don't you go get Stannum and Stibnum? They live very close together, so it isn't too much of a chore. Now, I have to arrange something, so who wants to get Hydrargyrum?"

The Chemy-lion's tail twitched. "The Human and I shall retrieve Mercury, which is closest to the Sun's demesnes."

"Fine, then," agreed Argentum. "See you all by the Chemistree." She trotted off and the group dispersed through the woods. Julie was left standing beside Al the Chemy-lion.

"Where are we going?" she queried.

"To Mercury."

"The planet?"

"His lands. They are next to the Sun's." The Chemy-lion sniffed the air for a moment, then set off through the woods, angling away from Ferrum's gate.

Julie shook her head, confused, and followed the Chemy-lion. "The planet Mercury is closest to the sun," she said.

The Chemy-lion spared her a single glance. "Not the planet."

"Then which Mercury? Surely the Periodic Mercury doesn't live here, because he's modern. His predecessor, you mean?"

The Chemy-lion nodded.

"Then why didn't you say so?" Julie grumbled. "And what is that business about the sun?"

"You have met the Sun."

"You mean, he's one of the Periodics I just met?"

The beast nodded again as he shifted between shades of gray, brown, and green, flowing through the forest like a living stream.

"Let me guess. Not Ferrum?"

"Not Mars," the Chemy-lion agreed.

Julie paused, then resumed: "Not Natrium?"

"Not Saturn," the lion agreed again. "The Sun is the perfect planet."

"The sun is not a planet!" Julie gave his irrational statement some thought. "And you said that gold was the perfect metal. So are you talking about Aurum?"

The lion nodded vigorously.

"Aurum is the sun? I still don't get it."

"Alchemical symbolism bequeaths certain metals with celestial nomenclature."

"In other words, Aurum *is* the sun. Who came up with all this?"

"Humans perform alchemical experiments."

"But why the planetary confusion?"

"Humans like to hide knowledge from each other. Alchemy is important knowledge to some."

Julie pondered that for a moment, then decided to change the subject. "Chemy?" she began.

"Yes?"

"Did any humans ever figure out how to make lead into gold — I mean, to make the Whatever-you-call-it Stone?"

The Chemy-lion smiled briefly but did not reply.

"Well? Did they?"

The Chemy-lion gave her a long, steady look and kept walking. "Alchemy is a very old science," he commented.

"Alchemy isn't a science," she objected.

"Alchemy *was* science, in its time."

The Chemy-lion had her there. Julie scratched her head.

The Chemy-lion cleared his throat, then delivered his first clear (and longest) sentence so far: "Whether or not Humans were able to produce the Philosopher's Stone is irrelevant, when it is seen how alchemical experimentation led to modern chemistry."

"How so?"

"Humans mix different chemicals together and observe what happens. Humans develop equipment to heat and cool their mixtures. Humans learn techniques and methods for chemistry."

The Chemy-lion cleared his throat again, and Julie interpreted that as a sign that she would get no more explanations from him right now. She decided to try once more anyway: "So that's what you meant when you said you had always led the way to the Chemistree. You were talking — sort of — about chemistry, the science, and how alchemy led up to it."

The lion flashed his fang-cornered smile again but did not answer. Julie assumed she was right.

"So Humans never found the Philosopher's Stone," she concluded.

"One did not say that." The lion's tail twitched slightly.

"Well, why didn't one just say 'yes' when I asked if they had?"

"Because a Human would inquire how."

"So?"

"Humans need to find out how for themselves."

"You'd just refuse to tell me." Julie put on her professional pout. The lion gave a curious-sounding sigh, shook his mane, and picked up the pace slightly.

They came to a path that ran nearly perpendicular to their line of travel and passed over it without pausing. They walked about the same length of time and came to another path. At this one, the Chemy-lion lowered his nose to the path, sniffed briefly, and turned left.

"These paths seem to be running parallel to each other," Julie commented. "If I didn't know better, I'd say they were set up like a grid ... or a table."

The Chemy paused only to nod, then continued on.

"Two paths over there was where Iron — ah, Ferrum — lived," Julie said, "and you just told me that Mercury lives next to Gold. I mean, their predecessors do. That's just like the elements are arranged on the Periodic Table."

The beast nodded again, trotting down the new path.

"So Aurum lives next to Mercury's predecessor because their atomic numbers are close together, huh? Just like on the real table. They're arranged by their numbers of itty-bitty protons."

The Chemy kept trotting, and Julie was having a hard time keeping up with him. Well, she'd just have to wait and see.

They passed a marvelous golden arch on the left, glimmering in the tree-juggled sunlight, and continued down the path for a short way. Then they came to a strange-looking puddle in the forest floor, also to the left of the path. The Chemy stopped.

Julie stepped up to the dark puddle and was shocked to see herself reflected – distorted around the edges – in its convex surface.

"A mirror!"

"Mercury," corrected the Chemy. He stepped around the puddle and padded among the trees on that side of the path. As Julie scuffed through the piled leaves, she exposed patches of bright orange sand. This had been a path at one time.

The leaf coating began to wear thin in places and the path became spotty orange. Julie saw something moving along the path up ahead and was surprised to see that it was a brook of mercury, sliding sinuously among the long-dead leaves.

"Look, Chemy!"

"Mercury," he repeated, without looking.

Julie paused for a moment to gaze at the shimmering stream slipping away beneath the trees. It seemed alive. It made no sound as it flowed, and its mirrored surface was unmarked by ripples. The outer edges of the stream projected up above the forest floor, convex like the puddle that marked the path. It was eerie. She peered along its length, where it curved away from the path into the trees, but the darkness obscured its course there. She wondered how far it went and where.

"Chemy," she called, and without waiting for a reply, "Where does this stream go?"

"The mercury stream flows back to its source, like the Ouroboros, sign of continuous life."

Julie let that perplexing comment pass for the moment, lost in contemplation of the glimmering current. It flowed faster than water, yet so smoothly that Julie had a hard time judging just how fast it was going. To test it, she plucked a half-decayed leaf from the ground, straightened it parallel to the surface, and placed it carefully on top of the stream. It zipped away, eliciting a gasp of surprise from her, then sank beneath the heavy surface.

"Chemy, this stream really flows!" she shouted.

"Quicksilver," called back the Chemy in explanation. He sounded far away.

Oh, that was right. Quicksilver was another name for mercury. Now Julie knew why they called it that. She turned and spotted the Chemy down the path, merged, as always, with the dark background.

She dashed across the intervening distance, watching the stream flow along the path, then curve away into the forest's shadows, and arrived beside her enigmatic companion somewhat out of breath.

"Chemy," she gasped, "what was that you said about the stream flowing back to its source?"

"The stream is like the Ouroboros, sign of eternal life," recited the beast, padding along on silent paws. A flash of color startled Julie, and she looked down to see the star-spotted black footprints being left behind. The Chemy noted her gaze and explained, "One thought the Human might need assistance in finding one again."

Julie looked back down the path and saw the black prints before the white-starred ones began. *He must always leave them in that order*, she mused. Then, aloud: "What's an ouroboros?"

"The sign of eternally renewed life, of birth and death, of reincarnation into a purer form. The Ouroboros takes the form of a great snake biting its own tail."

"Reincarnation? We're getting religious now?"

"Alchemy was a religion to some," mused the Chemy.

"Surely not to the Hindus! Isn't reincarnation part of Hinduism?"

The Chemy tossed his mane, apparently not knowing how to answer.

"Well, why is there an ouroboros-like stream made of mercury here?" she asked, going back to the original confusion.

The Chemy nodded to himself, shot her a look, and told her, "White Mercury, the feminine element of fluidity, works with Red Sulfur to form the Philosopher's Stone."

"You just told me the secret!" exclaimed Julie. "Even though I have no idea what you said...."

The Chemy smiled to himself. "Many know the constituents. Others know the process. But few can make the Philosopher's Stone."

"You said 'few.' That means some people have made it, doesn't it?" Julie crowed.

"One did not say that," the Chemy replied. Julie scowled.

"So the only reason the mercury stream forms a loop is so it's shaped like an ouroboros, because mercury is involved in making the Philosopher's Stone?"

The lion nodded affirmatively. "That," he admitted, "and because the stream had nowhere else to go."

Julie nearly screamed in frustration. Luckily, just then they rounded a bend and came to a wide stone archway, decorated with delicate gray foliage, down which a constant stream of mercury fell, covering the opening with a heavy curtain of liquid mirror.

"We can push through it, can't we?" inquired Julie dubiously.

"Many alchemists have perished from mercury poisoning in their experimentation," warned the Chemy.

"Mercury is poisonous?" Julie gasped.

"Even mercury's vapor, rising from the surface of the liquid, is poisonous."

"But I've been breathing it all along!" Julie was horrified.

"You are Human," pointed out the Chemy.

Julie's gaping mouth snapped shut. She knew that in Mathematics — and Science, she presumed — Humans had unusual powers. She just wasn't sure what they were yet. "Then I can walk on through, can't I?"

The Chemy shook his head, pacing toward the soundless waterfall.

"Why not?" Julie asked.

"Politeness before all else," he replied, and tugged on a bell-pull similar to the one at Ferrum's gate.

After a moment, the waterfall shut off. Mercury began coursing down the sides of the archway onto the ground, where it ran in narrow channels back behind the gate.

The Chemy-lion marched through the wide archway, which Julie now saw was the opening to a large tunnel formed of tightly-packed gray stone blocks. She trotted after him one pace behind, but he seemed eager now, and it was hard for Julie to keep up with him.

"Chemy, wait," she panted, but the lion did not hear her. His star-dotted prints faintly illuminated the smooth tunnel floor, and Julie was able to follow them out the other end. But when she emerged into the light, she saw that it was a gray half-light filtered through a dark gray, impenetrable ceiling of low clouds. In fact, most of the light seemed to come from the far corner of the clearing she was in, where the clouds ended abruptly and a peculiar round building squatted.

"Chemy," she called, running to catch up, "please wait!"

The Chemy did not seem to hear her. She scowled and hurried after him. It was no good trying to slow him down, so she might as well speed herself up.

She barely had time to look at the scenery as they rushed toward the building at the edge of the clearing. She saw that the orange path was flanked by twin quicksilver streams that rolled toward the tunnel. Beyond them were grass, peculiar grayish plants, and more forest, but she didn't have time to inspect any of them. Glancing at the odd building, she observed, "Isn't that an observatory?"

"It houses a telescope of sorts," replied the Chemy-lion.

"Isn't that the same thing?" she inquired, but before he could answer they had arrived at the entrance to the building. The Chemy clawed open the door, which slid sideways, and together they walked through the opening.

The interior was dark, and it took Julie's eyes a moment to adjust. When they did, she saw a vast, open chamber with a rounded ceiling. An angular instrument pointed toward the ceiling, and a short, circular wall filled over half of the floor space. In the middle of the room, stairs led up to a platform which held the instrument. Standing next to the instrument, using her mouth to fiddle with its controls, was a Periodic.

"... Got to get Ferrum over here to fix these steel knobs," the horse was muttering to herself around the knobs, in a barely intelligible voice. "... Don't know what I'm going to do with these. I —"

"Greetings, Mercury," purred the Chemy-lion, coming up behind her.

"Hydrargyrum," corrected the Periodic absently, not turning. Then she jumped. "Oh, yes. It's you, Chemy. I let you in." She turned around, sighted Julie, then glanced quizzically at the Chemy-lion. "A new pupil?"

"Julie does not learn the ways of alchemy," the Chemy asserted.

"What brings you here, Julie?" Hydrargyrum asked without preamble, eyeing her.

"There's a Council meeting," replied Julie respectfully. The Periodic was about the same size as Aurum, perhaps a little larger, and shone a dull gray color. Julie had no doubt that, were she in the sun, the Periodic would reflect light brilliantly in every direction.

Ex-Periodic, Julie corrected herself idly. Then: *Perhaps that's why there's such a cloud cover here, to keep Mercury — Hydrargyrum — from blinding all her guests. Or maybe it's a cloud of poisonous mercury vapor.* She shuddered.

"I see," responded the ex-Periodic without interest. She absently puffed her bangs-like forelock out of one eye and turned around.

"It's important," declared Julie. "It has to do with Wolfram."

Hydrargyrum paused, then sighed. "I knew that troublemaker would inconvenience us all sooner or later. When is the meeting?"

"In less than an hour."

"In about twenty minutes," amended the Chemy-lion.

"Twenty minutes!" Hydrargyrum stared at them in amazement. "But I have work to do!"

"Sorry," the beast murmured.

Hydrargyrum scowled, then brightened. "Julie, you're a Human. Do you think you could come up here and turn these knobs for me?"

"Sure." Julie ascended the wide stairs and glanced at the myriad controls before her. "Which ones?"

"Well, I need to turn this one ten degrees, that one sixty degrees, this one thirty degrees —"

"Okay, okay! One at a time." Julie twisted the narrow knobs as Hydrargyrum had indicated. She spent two or three more minutes following Hydrargyrum's directions, then turned around to gaze over the room, drying her hands on her jeans. Behind the circular wall, forming its peculiar convex shape, was a huge pool of mercury.

"What's that for?"

"What? Oh. When it's spun rapidly, the centrifugal force flattens the surface to an almost perfect mirror. It reflects the stars much better that way."

"Do Humans know about this?"

"Sure. They came up with it. I'm very proud. My successor brought the idea to me just last year, and I've been playing around in here ever since."

"What do you look at?"

"The planet Mercury, what else?" The former Periodic laughed and descended the stairs. "Let's make haste, Chemy. We haven't much time."

"Wait!" exclaimed Julie. "If you run, I won't be able to keep up with you."

The Chemy coughed delicately. "You could carry her on your back," he pointed out to Hydrargyrum.

"What? I'm not a beast of burden."

"It wouldn't do any harm. She's very light, I'm sure."

"Well, not as light as I was when Kalium carried me," admitted Julie, "but I don't weigh a ton, either."

"You rode on Kalium's back? Whatever possessed her to let you do such a thing?"

"Well, Potassium carried me to her. She was supposed to keep an eye on me until the Periodic Council met, the last time I was here."

Hydrargyrum eyed her dubiously. "Well, if Kalium can do it, I suppose I can, too. Overlooking the fact that she's nearly twice my size." She approached the stairs. "Get on."

Julie took a deep breath, leaned out over the stairs, and swung her leg over the former Periodic's broad back. She shifted her center of balance until it was over her reluctant steed, letting her other leg drop down. Then she tentatively squeezed with her knees. "I haven't ridden a horse very often," she told Hydrargyrum. "Only a few times in my world, and here, when I came to Mathematics. The last time I was here was a while ago."

"I'll make an effort not to let you fall off," the former Periodic promised. "Now let's go."

"At a walk," suggested Julie, "then a canter, then a gallop?"

"If you insist," Hydrargyrum sighed.

3
The Council of the Periodics Emeriti

THEY ARRIVED at the Chemistree clearing just as Argentum was calling the meeting to order. Julie was out of breath even though she hadn't been running. The rush of wind and blur of forest had nearly overwhelmed her as they raced toward the meeting at top speed. Hydrargyrum ran easily as fast as a race horse, possibly even as fast as a cheetah. The Chemy, always a fraction of an inch ahead of them, matched her stride for stride.

Quicksilver, thought Julie wryly, as she slid to the ground.

"Here's our Human!" announced Aurum cheerfully as Julie staggered toward the center of the clearing.

The assembled former Periodics all turned their heads to gaze curiously at her.

"We don't get many of them around here," mused a small

silver-white horse, whose archaic-lettered "Sb" made Julie wonder who her modern successor was. The letters were unfamiliar.

"Okay, so what's up?" inquired her apparent twin — except for the substitution of "Sn" instead of "Sb" — in a male voice. Julie wasn't sure who he was, either.

"It's Tungsten," Julie began hesitantly. "I know there's been trouble around here with him — I heard talk the last time I was here, and I was attacked by wolframs because I am a human. But today in my world —"

"Julie!" exclaimed a familiar voice from behind her. She spun around to see Natrium, the small gray former Periodic she had met earlier, and her old friend Kalium. It was the latter who had spoken.

"Kalium!" she cried, running to her side. Kalium was taller than Natrium, and her fur was thicker, and she seemed heavier as well. But Julie knew they were "Group-mates," as Lithium had once told her, because their modern successors were both in Group IA on the Periodic Table — the Alkali Metals.

"What are you doing here?" Kalium asked, overjoyed. She nuzzled Julie's hair while Julie clung to her neck.

"That's what I was about to tell the Council." Julie drew back reluctantly and faced the curious former Periodics again. There was important business to take care of. "In my world today, all the tungsten stopped operating. It just doesn't do what it's supposed to. The X-ray machines, the light bulbs, everything. I thought it might mean there was trouble here, so I opened a portal using my Chemistry book and came to see if I could help."

"Chemistry," noted the Chemy, nodding toward the gigantic tree. Julie gazed up at it in wonder, suddenly realizing that her Chemistry book had brought her indirectly to the Chemistree. Coincidence? Julie was inclined to think not.

"But how can all the tungsten just stop working?" Julie queried. "I mean, I know the Periodics have control of their elements here in Mathematics — Science, I mean — but I thought you didn't have any control in my world."

"Implied Permission," commented Aurum.

"What?"

Aurum crossed to the humongous bole and poked his nose into the opening. "Come get out the book," he requested. Julie obligingly went to his side and lifted out the heavy tome, placing it in the grass. The Chemy greened sinuously over to them and sniffed at the worn pages.

"Implied Permission," repeated Aurum, nosing open the book and carefully licking the pages over.

"Here, let me do that," offered Julie, lifting up sections of the pages for him. "Tell me when to stop. You know, you guys really ought to have hands or something. Why don't you take human form?"

"We can't," protested Aurum. "Stop!"

Julie smoothed the requested page over. "This is what I was reading earlier!" she exclaimed. She looked at the entry dated June 14, 1849, which discussed how the former Periodic Aurum ("That's *you!*" she said to Aurum) had wished to deny Implied Permission in her world.

"Why did you want to do that?" she asked.

Aurum grimaced. "Have you ever heard of the Forty-Niners?"

"The Gold Rush in California? Sure. I learned about that in history class."

"That's why."

Julie scratched her head. "You didn't like the Gold Rush?"

"Of course not! I mean, it's bad enough that Humans consider me such a precious metal, but when they go into a frenzy trying to find me.... That's going too far."

"So what would have happened if you had denied the Implied Permission to them?"

"The gold in their world would have stopped being gold. It would have lost all of its chemical and physical properties. Unless I were standing right there watching, or I gave someone specific permission to use my element."

Julie thought about that. "What would that entail? I mean, obviously the gold wouldn't combine with any other elements, because that's a chemical property, but how can something lose its physical properties? I mean, what color would it be? What about its boiling point and melting point?"

"It would be no color. It would have no boiling point and no melting point."

"How can that be? What state of matter would it be in? I mean, most elements are solid at room temperature because their melting points are well above room temperature ... except for mercury, of course." Julie glanced at Hydrargyrum. "Come to think of it, some elements are gas at room temperature. But

45

that's beside the point. If an element had no melting point, it wouldn't be solid *or* liquid *or* gas. What would it be?"

"I don't know," admitted Aurum. "No one's ever denied Permission before."

"There are four states of matter," remarked Kalium thoughtfully. "Plasma is the fourth."

Julie gasped. "But plasma is what the sun is made of! It's only found at very, very high temperatures!"

Kalium shrugged, which was an interesting thing to see a horse do. "I have no answer for you."

"So do you think that's what Wolfram has done? Denied Implied Permission in my world?"

The other Periodics looked disgruntled. "Well, he'd have to let us vote on it in Council," the female "Sb" replied, finally. "He wouldn't do so otherwise."

"Wouldn't or couldn't?" Julie inquired shrewdly.

The horses looked grim. "Wouldn't," admitted Argentum at last, "simply because we've always relayed these things to the Council so we can work together. It's altogether possible that he could if he wanted to."

"Sb" jumped. "Not without Tungsten's permission!" she exclaimed.

"She's right," reflected "Sn." "Tungsten would have to let him do it."

"Stibnum, Stannum, you have a good point," Argentum told them. Julie was relieved to know their names at last, although she still couldn't tell who their modern counterparts were.

"Could Tungsten be working with Wolfram?" Stibnum asked.

"It's hard to say," mused Argentum. "Kalium, have you spoken with Tungsten lately?"

Kalium was shaking her head even before the question was asked. "Tungsten's been making trouble beyond the Elemental Forest. His wolframs have been attacking centers of power inside Mathematics."

"Wolfram always had those pet wolframs!" Hydrargyrum exclaimed. "Tungsten never had any!"

"He does now," Kalium asserted. "And he's using them to take over Mathematics."

The former Periodics fell silent, and they all looked troubled.

"We'd better go there," Argentum conceded at last. "We need to find out what's going on."

"If Tungsten and Wolfram have taken over Mathematics, the Mathematician will need our help," Julie said.

The Chemy nodded solemnly. Julie realized that he and the Mathematician were probably old companions, because alchemy and higher mathematics were developed around the same time. At least, she thought they were.

"We shouldn't waste any time, then," Kalium stated. "Julie, get on my back."

Julie looked up at her friend, then around at the others.

"Can somebody lift me up?" she asked.

"Climb the tree," suggested Stannum.

Julie looked in the direction he indicated and saw a large evergreen tree with several low branches nearly parallel to the ground. It wouldn't be too hard to climb. She did so, getting sap on her hands, and swung onto her friend's back.

"Who's going and who's not going?" Hydrargyrum asked as Julie wiped her hands futilely on her jeans. By now those pants were looking pretty stained.

"I'll walk as far as the edge of the forest," offered Stannum, "but the Humans are trying a new way of extracting tin from ore and I really wanted to be there...."

"Okay, okay," Kalium said. "Let's just get going."

They moved out at a canter down the path that had brought Julie to the clearing. She suddenly realized that, had she walked in the opposite direction, she would have left the forest altogether.

The Chemy raced at Kalium's side, a blur of grays and browns over the rutted pathway.

"Stannum," she called, as they went along, "are you Tin's predecessor?"

"I sure am," Stannum replied.

"That means you have eight isotopes."

Stannum looked surprised. "Well, yes and no. They became Tin isotopes when I was replaced.... And that's only counting the natural ones.... But how did you know that?"

"Potassium told me last time I was here. It sort of stuck." Julie tapped at her forehead.

"My brother has a penchant for scientific explanations," Kalium explained to Stannum. "I guess it runs in the family. He was explaining atomic mass and isotopes at the time, I believe."

"Oh." Stannum eyed her. "So when did the tungsten stop working in your world?"

"Tonight. Suddenly the lights in my room stopped working, and I heard a news report that all the X-ray machines had stopped working, too, and were shooting radiation out."

Stannum nodded. "Yep. That would happen. A tungsten target inside those machines slows those electrons down, so that ordinarily they produce X-rays. Oh, what a mess! It sure sounds like he's denied Permission, all right."

Julie looked at Stannum's seeming twin, who was running beside him. "Who is your successor?" she inquired.

"Antimony," replied Stibnum. "A metalloid."

"That means she's neither metal nor nonmetal? Somewhere in between?" Julie just wanted to check her inventory of chemical facts. After all, she might need them in the impending struggle against Tungsten.

"Right."

Cuprum came up behind her. He was somewhat shorter than Kalium — about the same height as Stibnum — so he had to call up to her: "Julie, did the malfunctioning X-ray machines produce any plasma?"

"I hope not! They'd melt the machines and the hospital, and everything else, too, I imagine. But why?"

"Well, if they did, that confirms the theory that an element, once denied Permission, becomes plasma. But I guess it doesn't."

The Chemy chuckled.

"What's funny?" asked Julie, but the Chemy refused to answer.

They traveled for over an hour at the easygoing rate, and Julie soon got bored with watching the scenery slide by.

"Kalium?" she began.

"Yes?"

"How is everyone? Lithium, and Hydrogen, Tritium, and Deuterium? How's Al?"

"They're all fine. I haven't seen Al in quite a while, though. The Mathematician has him on some assignment, I think. Or maybe just running errands."

Julie nodded.

"I hope the Mathematician is all right," worried Kalium. "Wolfram is quite insane."

"Tungsten's insane, too," put in Plumbum, who was cantering beside Hydrargyrum. The latter glanced at him questioningly. "He's got to be," Plumbum explained. "He's working with Wolfram, isn't he?"

"We don't know that," stated Argentum. "Wolfram could have captured him. And forced him to deny Permission."

"How? Tungsten holds the office. He has more power than Wolfram, and he's younger and stronger."

Argentum looked at Plumbum. "Wolfram has his wolframs," she pointed out.

"That's a good point."

"So the wolframs are either working for Wolfram and against Tungsten, or for them both?" Kalium clarified.

"Yes." Argentum twitched one ear. "Either way, it's not a pretty sight. Periodics shouldn't fight each other."

"When did Wolfram disappear?" inquired Julie, remembering what Argentum had told her.

"Several months ago," replied Kalium. "In fact, somewhat before you arrived here the first time."

"So as soon as he disappeared, the wolframs began making trouble in Mathematics."

Kalium nodded. "You're right. But I didn't know he'd disappeared until two days ago, when I returned to my old haunts. And then it just never registered."

They were heading west now, on a narrower path where the trees crowded close and the shadows stretched long behind them.

"How long before we get to Mathematics?" Julie inquired.

"Probably another day," replied Kalium. "We're traveling at a fair pace, but it's a long way."

Julie frowned. All of a sudden, she wished she had a car — or even a motorcycle.

"What if we go faster?" she asked.

"We'd get there faster," replied Kalium laconically.

"Well, why can't we?"

"We could, but it wouldn't do any good. I want to talk to the Periodic Council, and that's not for three more days."

"Why do we need to talk to them?"

"So we can find out the latest about Tungsten and/or Wolfram, and so I can tell them it's Wolfram behind the trouble, possibly alone. Remember, they still think it's Tungsten."

"Oh." Julie looked around at the shadowy forest. "But aren't we going to Mathematics first? Shouldn't we hurry?"

Hydrargyrum overheard her. "What's this?" she inquired, coming up behind them.

Kalium turned toward Hydrargyrum. "Hyd, I want to talk to the Council before we go on to Mathematics. That way we can find out what's happened."

Hydrargyrum made an equine scowl. "That's up to you. You can go to the Council if you want, but I'd rather not."

Chemy looked up at Kalium. "Alchemy leads first to mathematics, then to science," he warned.

"In other words, he wants to go to see the Mathematician first," Julie translated. "Which is what I think we should do, too."

At this point, several of her new friends began to argue about where they were headed, and they came to a standstill on the path. Kalium asserted in no uncertain terms that they were going to the Council first, while the Chemy demanded circuitously that they see the Mathematician. A large contingent expressed the view that they didn't want to go to either, while a couple threatened to return to the Chemistree.

"Stop this! Stop this!" shouted Argentum eventually. "We must not fight! That's what Tungsten and Wolfram started!"

A strange silence fell over the group. Then Julie suggested, "Let's take a vote."

"That's a good idea," remarked Argentum.

"Well, I live in a democracy," Julie stated modestly, giggling.

So they voted. The majority opted for going to the Council first, so the group continued west through the ever-lengthening shadows toward the clearing where Julie had seen the Periodic Council during her first visit.

As the shadows overlapped each other and their surroundings softened into gray, Kalium called a halt. "We're really not in any rush," she pointed out.

The Chemy twitched his tail in response, looking around alertly. It seemed that he could see perfectly well in the dark.

"Do you think we should light a fire?" Argentum asked.

"Yes," responded Natrium, Stannum, and Stibnum in unison. They were also looking around, but Julie knew they could not see as well as the Chemy. They were all nervous.

Her friends' agitation affected Julie, and she, too, began to feel uneasy. She slipped down from Kalium's back and seated herself next to the Chemy, arranging several large stones in a rough circle for the fire.

"How are we going to light it?" Julie inquired.

"Alchemy shall light the way," the Chemy purred, his deep voice rumbling up from beside Julie's head, where the furry chest rose and fell.

"Okay. How are you going to do that?"

The Chemy chuckled, a characteristic sound now. "Humans still seek the secrets of alchemy!"

"Fine, then," Julie said, in mock indignation. "Don't tell me."

"Humans shall discover for themselves," the Chemy growled good-naturedly.

"I'll get some wood," Aurum offered. He began picking up twigs from the ground with his teeth and throwing them into the stone circle Julie had made. The others joined in and soon Julie had a veritable brush-pile, complete with leaves.

"That's enough! That's enough!" she exclaimed, pulling some out. "I need bigger pieces!"

Ferrum complied by dragging a fallen branch down the path, which he then cracked into usable chunks by smashing one fore-hoof down on it.

Once the wood was arranged into a rough teepee, making it look like a tiny Plains Indian had moved in and built a wall of boulders around his home, the Chemy sat gazing at it contemplatively. Julie watched him for several minutes but nothing happened. A chill wind brushed past her face, swinging a few strands of hair into her eyes. She turned to glance at the others, brushing the hair aside as she did, and saw a faint flicker of light wash over the group. When she whirled around, there was fire clinging to the upper part of the teepee, chewing down into it merrily.

"You did that on purpose!" Julie accused the Chemy, but there was no reply, just a smug smile.

They sat around the fire that night, basking in the warmth against the increasingly chill darkness. Not long after the fire was lit, Julie discovered that she was famished. All the excitement had kept her from feeling hunger, but now her stomach had caught up to her. She dug into her bag and drew out the dried fruit, munching as her friends murmured around her and fed on some grass growing nearby. Later that night, as Julie stretched out between the Chemy and Kalium, she realized that they had left no one on watch. That was her last clear thought before her mind sank into oblivion.

4
The Howling Darkness

JULIE AWOKE to a high-pitched wailing that instantly sent waves of ice down her spine: *"Human! Human! Human!"*

The wolframs had come!

Julie opened her eyes, but there was only more darkness. Her heart lurched and she tried to claw away whatever was over her face, but she found she couldn't move at all. Terror replaced her fear.

The darkness shifted beside her and a deep rumbling began. Julie, as frightened as she was, took new fear from the terrible, angry sound. The rumbling increased in volume, swelling into a powerful roar. It was the Chemy.

The cries of "Human! Human!" had disappeared when the roar finally fell silent. In the sudden quiet, Julie could hear her heart pounding in her eardrums. She trembled and felt a massive paw drape over her stomach.

"Humans should not fear the darkness," rumbled the Chemy, as a flicker of light built somewhere over Julie's head, "but only the fears that lurk within."

"Tell that to the wolframs," Julie muttered, trying to move again. She was still paralyzed by some unknown force. "Why can't I move?"

"You are bound in bonds of base metal," the Chemy replied.

"Tungsten?"

"Yes."

"The wolframs did this?"

"Yes."

"Where are they now?"

"The base metal shudders in the presence of fire, runs, then flies."

"What?" Julie knew there was more to what the Chemy had just said, but she couldn't quite comprehend it. Runs? Flies? Fire would melt metal, making it liquid … making it run … then … would metal vaporize? Julie's confused mind skipped around the concept. Surely it would, if the fire were hot enough. Then the metallic gas would "fly" in clouds. So that's what the Chemy had meant! In one sense, the Chemy had said that the wolframs ran away from the fire — or from him — but in a deeper sense, he had told her that metals would vaporize. Julie was feeling proud of herself — she was starting to understand the cryptic messages he proclaimed. And that was saying something.

The Chemy shifted his weight slightly, focusing his emerald gaze at Julie's pinned arms. Suddenly she could move again.

With relief, she rolled over, getting to her knees and throwing a hug around the lion's neck. "How did you do that?" she asked.

"Alchemy involves a complex change of state of matter," the Chemy replied.

"So you can melt the metal bonds I had on?" Julie asked.

The Chemy nodded sagely.

"Where are the others?" Julie half-turned to see her equine companions bound immobile in thick metal bands, including one around their muzzles.

The Chemy stood and paced toward them, his tail twitching. As he drew nearer, the metal bands began to sag, then drip, and run in rivulets off her friends' skin. Julie was amazed. The Chemy had phenomenal power!

"How do you do that?" Stibnum wanted to know, shaking his head back and forth as if to assure himself that he was truly free.

The Chemy's chuckle drifted across the clearing. "The Mathematician achieves his goals through working the equations to get the solution he desires. He knows the mathematical processes by which to manipulate the matter with which he works. So, too, does alchemy have a specific process, which one comprehends." The Chemy's pause indicated that the "one" was himself. "One merely has to follow it."

Julie sighed. Her luck in translating the Chemy's meaning was running out. His last speech had been far above her head.

Aurum was scowling. "How did we get caught unaware like that?" He glared in the direction the wolframs had fled.

"We didn't leave a watch," Argentum replied. "It was our own folly. We are lucky the wolframs only tied us up. It could have been much worse."

"The wolframs wouldn't dare harm us," Hydrargyrum stated. "They know us, and they know we're just as powerful as Wolfram is."

"Maybe," growled someone behind Julie.

They spent the rest of the night in a tight knot, unable to sleep — except for Aurum, who snoozed blissfully with Julie's backpack cradled between his forelegs. His metallic color dimmed into deepest brown in the darkness, yellow and orange spreading across his back and side as he breathed in the firelight.

$$\female \quad \leftmoon \quad \male \quad \triangledown \quad \mercury \quad \earth$$

When morning came, everyone was irritable — except for Aurum, who got snapped at so many times that he, too, became peevish. They made their way between the trees, still heading west, on a path that grew more and more narrow and ill-kempt the farther they went. Anxious about an ambush, they all spent much of the time looking over their shoulders.

"I can't believe this!" exclaimed Stannum, as they paused for lunch. "I can't believe we're actually afraid of those foolish wolframs. I mean, they were always a nuisance, but a danger . . . never."

"Times change," responded Argentum dryly. The Chemy nodded in agreement, looking rather glum.

It was just before sunset when they heard hoofbeats coming down the path toward them. The only reason they heard the sound was because they had paused to drink from a small brook, and they were so worn out that no one was chatting. The Chemy heard it first and jerked his head up. One by one, the horses did the same. Finally Julie heard the muffled *thump-thump-thump* in the ground that explained her companions' looks.

"Who do you think it is?" someone asked.

"Don't know," replied someone else in a whisper. "Maybe one of the current Periodics."

"I hope they're not bringing bad news," Argentum sighed.

Suddenly, not far down the path, there came a terrible howling and yelping. The ruckus sounded like it was just around the bend.

"That sounds like a whole pack of wolframs!" Cuprum exclaimed, galloping toward the noise.

"Let's help whoever it is," cried Stannum as he took off as well.

Julie ran after the group of horses, but they outdistanced her in seconds. As their powerful hindquarters and swinging tails disappeared around the bend, the fierce cries of the wolframs turned into yelps of pain and fear. Julie continued after them, but the Chemy leaped down from a tree, landing inches from her. She jumped in fright, almost skidding into him, and shouted, "Chemy!"

"Apologies," purred the beast, twitching his tail. "Humans should not be unescorted when wolframs are about."

Julie sighed, knowing he was right. "What's going on?" she asked as she started to run again. The Chemy trotted beside her.

"Equine beasts can kick fierce but foolish wolframs into the dust," replied the Chemy with his typical unhelpfulness.

Julie kept running toward the sounds of yelping, stomping, shouting, and howling. As she rounded the bend, she saw each of her equine friends facing off against one or more wolframs, using sharp, hard hooves and teeth to hold back the snarling brutes. They were grouped around a fallen figure that was draped in a large, emerald-green cloth. Julie spared the sad-looking pile a single glance before her attention was jerked to a wolfram that bounded out in front of her, baring its fangs in her face. The Chemy slashed out at it with naked claws, and the wolfram gave a yelp as it was cuffed across the head. It rolled over twice and fled, but soon returned with two others to attack the Chemy in a concerted effort that took his full attention. Meanwhile, a fourth wolfram muscled its way between Julie and her feline guardian, causing her to back away in fear. A quick glance around confirmed her suspicions. None of her other friends could help her; they were all occupied.

She cast about for some kind of weapon and sighted a short, stout branch lying nearby. She scooped it up as the wolfram made a rush toward her, and brought it up in time to jab at the wolfram's face. She missed, but it ducked away anyway. It gave an angry snarl, wheeling, and came in for a second rush, but this time Julie was better prepared. Jumping aside, she swung the branch like a baseball bat — and the wolfram's snout became the ball. Julie made contact with a satisfying *thunk.*

The wolfram hadn't lost all its fight, however. Julie backed up a few more steps, trying to hold on to her courage, and her heel pushed against something solid. She glanced back and saw the green blanket. The fallen figure, whoever or whatever it was, was behind her. She would either have to step over it, putting herself off-balance, or stand here until the wolfram attacked again.

As it turned out, the wolfram made her decision for her. While she had been distracted, it had been viciously kicking dirt up with its hind feet and snarling as if to prove to itself that it was tough. Now it threw itself at her once more. Bracing herself, Julie gritted her teeth and readied her makeshift club — and the wolfram, just as it got within range, was kicked backwards twenty feet by a powerful, equine leg coming from behind her!

Julie blinked and looked down at the leg, which was now resting on the ground before her. It was black-and-white striped, like a zebra's. No — the black marks were numbers — equations! It was —

"A gebra's ... ," she heard a pant from behind her, "... legs are stronger than a wolfram's any day."

"Al!" she cried, recognizing her friend's voice. She whirled and threw her arms around the gebra's broad black-and-white neck, now protruding from beneath the blanket.

"I was ambushed," Al panted, "and I was trying to catch my breath before helping my rescuers fight off these wolframs.

Awful beasts." Al's ears dipped backwards toward his erect, striped mane, then perked forward toward Julie again. "And how have you been?" His equine smile, unique to Mathematics, lightened Julie's heart.

"I'm great now!" she exclaimed. "It's so good to see you, Al gebra." She planted a delicate kiss on the gebra's dark nose, and his eyes crossed trying to track her actions. His smile widened and, with a surge, Al got to his feet.

"Same," the gebra returned, squeezing her to his front with one upraised foreleg. "Now let's help the Periodics Emeriti to fight what's left."

Julie glanced around at her friends, but they all seemed to have handled their wolframs with typical — as far as she had seen — facility. Several wolframs lay smashed into the dust, whimpering, and a significant number had fled the scene — in the same direction the group was traveling, from what she could tell by the faint yips and barks.

"Al gebra," Kalium greeted him gravely. "Greetings."

"Glorious morning," the gebra replied.

"Where did you manage to scoop up such a mangy collection of canines?" Natrium inquired, his equine eyebrows — such as they were — arching with humor.

"They've been following me from the Composite Plain in Mathematics," Al answered. "Sometimes far in the distance, sometimes so close I could make out the details of their ruffs. But I don't think they'll bother me anymore." He cast a defiant glance around the trampled path.

Julie looked around. As she watched, it seemed that Ferrum was, very slightly and almost indiscernibly, getting smaller.

"Ferrum," she called, trying to think of a tactful way to phrase her question, "are you ... shrinking?"

"Yes," replied Ferrum.

"We all are," Argentum told her.

"Um ... why?"

The Periodics looked amused. "Well, you might say we were in ... a hot situation," Kalium stated. "Heat makes elements expand, you know, so we ... expanded."

"You get larger when exposed to danger?" Julie scratched her head.

"It's not the danger," Argentum asserted. "It's the heat we generate in response to the situation. Or something like that."

Julie scowled. Her friends were even stranger than she had thought! Not only that, but they didn't seem as scientifically precise as their modern counterparts. "Or something like that" would never have come out of Hydrogen's mouth, or any of her isotopes', or any of the modern Periodics'.

"And I suppose being under pressure makes you smaller," Julie commented with some exasperation.

"Exactly!" Kalium replied.

Julie shook her head. She hadn't really expected an answer; her remark had been meant as a joke. "Then why didn't you shrink?" she asked.

"Because we weren't under a lot of pressure," Argentum answered. "Personally, I don't really fear the wolframs or think much of them. So I was under no pressure, just the heat of battle." She paused, lifting her delicate muzzle to the crisp air.

Julie sighed to herself, turning back to Al. Everything had a scientific explanation! That's what she got for visiting Science, she supposed. "So how are things in Mathematics, Al?" she inquired.

"Not so great," the gebra replied. "In fact, I'm an envoy for the Mathematician, sent to seek you out ... not you specifically, Julie, but the Periodics Emeriti —"

"What does that mean? Periodics Emeriti?" Julie interrupted.

"It's a respectful way of addressing the former Periodics," Al told her. "'Emeriti' is the plural of 'Emeritus.' It's like an adjective, meaning 'former,' put after their other title."

"Oh."

Al continued, suddenly formal: "The Mathematician requests the presence of the Periodics Emeriti in Higher Mathematics, to aid and advise him in the war against Tungsten, the insane member of your group."

"Then the Mathematician is still healthy and safe?" Aurum asked.

Al swiveled his ears toward the golden Periodic Emeritus. "Yes."

"Good tidings," purred the Chemy from next to Julie.

Al jumped, surprised to find anyone there but Julie. Neither of them had heard the Chemy approach.

"Al," Julie laid one hand on his neck and the other on the Chemy's thick mane, about neck-height to her, "this is the Chemy. His name is Al, too."

"Albertus," the beast said firmly.

"Al Chemy," Al murmured. "I have never heard of you. Where do you live?"

"Alchemy is an art of the past. There I live, in the hearts and minds of Humans long gone."

The gebra looked confused.

"He lives here, in the Forest," Argentum added helpfully. "He likes to talk that way."

Al nodded, then turned to Julie. "Would you like to ride on my back?"

Julie laughed at his eagerness. "Sure!"

He knelt in the dust and Julie swung one leg over his fuzzy back. *It's just like old times,* she mused contentedly as he surged to his feet and commenced walking back the way he had come. They spread out in a long line, a small group clustered at the front around Al and Julie. The Chemy faded back into the growth at the edge of the path, and Julie soon lost track of him.

$$♀ ☽ ♂ ▽ ☿ ⊕$$

"I'm very glad I found you," Al the gebra stated, "besides the fact that you saved my life. It's shortened my journey a great deal. But why were you traveling?"

"Because we were worried about the Mathematician," Julie answered. "Wolfram is apparently very dangerous now that he's unstable."

"Wolfram?" Al's ears perked back toward her. "You mean Tungsten."

"Well...." Julie took a deep breath. "How do I explain this? Kalium? Argentum?"

Argentum formulated the reply: "It was always Wolfram that had control of the wolframs," she stated. "We believe that, because of their presence, it means that either Wolfram and Tungsten are in league, or that Wolfram has somehow assumed his – Tungsten's – rightful powers again. Either way, we are concerned."

"It could also be that Tungsten is forcing Wolfram to make his wolframs do as he wants," Cuprum added.

Al nodded. "When is the last time Wolfram was seen?"

The Periodics Emeriti all paused for thought, cocking their respective heads.

"Months ago," Hydrargyrum replied.

"Just before Julie appeared the first time," Kalium added.

"And before he disappeared, he and his wolframs stayed locked up on his property, not coming out even for the occasional meeting we held," Stibnum added.

"Yes, for once my plants were safe," grumbled Hydrargyrum. "I hope he doesn't come back!"

"Hyd!" Stibnum exclaimed. "How could you say that?"

"Easily."

"Now, now," Argentum interceded, cutting off Stibnum's sharp reply, "we don't need to argue about that. He's coming back. Just as soon as he's cured of his insanity."

"Which means never," Hydrargyrum added.

"We don't know that he's incurable," Natrium put in. "He could just be under Tungsten's control."

"I guess that blows our vote," Kalium sighed. "I suppose we're going to the Mathematician now instead of to the Council."

"I thought we were following the wolframs," Aurum put in.

The others erupted into a new argument over their destination. Julie, hearing a reiteration of the old problem, sighed. "Let's take another vote," she suggested.

"Vote, nothing," Plumbum growled, "I'm following those wolframs back to Wolfram, and I'm going to give him a piece of my mind!"

"Here, here!" Hydrargyrum cheered. "Let's drag his hide back where it belongs!"

Argentum seemed upset at the prospect of violence. "But I thought you didn't *want* him back," she said, flustered.

"It's better to have him back here than running wild and endangering everyone," Hydrargyrum affirmed. Julie saw several heads nodding behind her.

"Who votes for following?" Julie asked tentatively.

"I do!" cried several voices.

"And for going to the Council?"

No one answered, not even Kalium.

"And for following Al back to the Mathematician?"

There was a small, half-hearted chorus of voices. Al angled his head back toward Julie. "Do I have a vote?"

"Sure."

"Then I say let's check in with the Mathematician first."

The Chemy phased out of the undergrowth just then. "Follow tracks when tracks are fresh," he asserted.

"No! We need to ask the Mathematician what to do!" Al expressed.

The Chemy sat down in the leaves. "One, now assured of the Mathematician's safety, says to find the source of the problem. One will not go to see for oneself. One will seek the problem."

"... Which means he's not going to the Mathematician," Julie translated for Al.

Al swished his tail with agitation and shifted his weight back and forth. "And most of you are for that?"

"It seems so," Kalium told him.

"Julie, what do you think we ought to do?" asked Al.

"I trust the Chemy's judgment," she said.

"Oh, please!" cried Cuprum with exasperation. "Can't we agree on anything? I'm going home!"

"No, don't do that!" cried Kalium.

Cuprum did not reply. Julie watched the shadows play over his brilliant orange back as he trotted away from the group.

"Stop, Cuprum," she bade him. "Please follow the trail for a while!"

"Why should I?" Cuprum demanded.

"At least see in which direction the wolframs go. Don't leave now!"

Cuprum glanced back down the path and toward her again. "Why not?"

"Because I want you to stay," she replied meekly, for lack of anything better to say.

To her surprise, Cuprum wheeled and returned to the group, although he looked reluctant.

"A Human's request is as good as an order," Al murmured to her, "even to a Periodic Emeritus. They've been utilized by Humans so long, it's second nature for them to do what one wants."

"I suppose it couldn't hurt," Cuprum grumbled as they resumed walking.

$$♀ ☾ ♂ ▽ ☿ ⊕$$

They stayed on the wolframs' trail for hours. It followed the path north, seeming to head toward the Periodic Council.

"That's so strange," Julie heard Kalium murmur once.

"Why?"

"It's almost as if they're going to the Council on purpose," Kalium replied, realizing with a start that she had been overheard.

They didn't even stop when it got dark, fearing what the wolframs might do if given enough time. They followed the beasts all night, Julie gnawing at the last of her dried fruit to hold off her hunger. When the sun rose through the dense trees, they came to the outer edge of the Elemental Forest, where the modern Periodics lived, which was marked by a ring of paper lanterns hung in the trees. There the paths became packed dirt and it was difficult to discern where the wolframs had been.

It wasn't too difficult, however. There came a sharp scream — feminine — off among the trees to the right. The group, clustered uncertainly where a path marked "Hydrogen" branched from the main path, now flew down that side-path to follow the sound.

"It's Hydrogen they're after," panted Kalium, jumping to a conclusion.

A small, flickering shape jumped out of the woods ahead of them, bracing its front legs against the impact, and galloped, panting, in the same direction they were headed.

"Hydrogen!" it — he — called desperately. "Deu! Trite! This way!"

Two more small shapes broke from the forest. Through them, Julie could see trees and brush flash by. The translucent shapes galloped headlong after the first.

"After them, Al!" she cried, and the gebra put on a sudden burst of speed. Julie clutched at his mane as the woods blurred. Beside them, the Chemy ran in great leaps, and the Periodics Emeriti raced just behind.

They came to a small glade, where a pack of wolframs had fallen upon the three shapes. Hydrogen was nowhere to be seen.

"Where's Hydrogen?" Kalium called, leaping into the fray with her front hooves flashing.

"They've taken her!" cried one of the three figures, kicking backwards with all his strength. It was a small horse.

Julie started to slide off Al's back, but he suddenly shook his head. "You're safest here," he asserted. "I'll stay out of the fight to protect you." There was genuine concern in his voice, so Julie heeded his words.

It seemed to take forever to drive off the wolframs this time. Julie watched in anxiety. Several of her friends sustained bites in the fray, but no one gave up until the wolframs had run howling into the woods.

The three small horses were thanking their unexpected saviors when Julie at last slid to the damp leaves and ran across the glade toward them.

"Deuterium! Tritium!" she called. The horses turned around.

"Julie!" they cried together. "What are you doing here?" Deuterium added.

"Following the wolframs," she replied, throwing her arms around their necks and burying her face in their soft fur. The third horse came up behind her and sniffed at her hair.

"A Human?" he asked, sounding puzzled.

"This Human's name is Julie. We journeyed with her to the Mathematician once," Deuterium told him. "Julie, this is our Isotope-brother Protium."

Julie turned to look at him. Protium grinned at her, bent one foreleg, and bowed with practiced grace. "I'm fond of Humans," he said.

Julie was charmed by this self-possessed little horse. She bowed to him in turn. "Pleased to meet you, Protium," she replied.

"We've got to help Hydrogen," Tritium said. "The wolframs took her, then fought us off to keep us from following."

"They have so much of a lead now, we might as well talk to the Council," Deuterium said woefully.

For once the Periodics Emeriti agreed as a body. "We need backup," Aurum stated. He fixed his calm gray eyes on the woods the wolframs had torn through — with their captive.

5
The Second Council and a Second Journey

THE COUNCIL was set to meet later that night, so Julie and her companions ate with the worried Isotopes and slept on soft moss beds in the shade of the overhanging trees. When Julie awoke, the sun was so low in the sky that the tree trunks blocked most of its light. Protium, Deuterium, and Tritium were hanging more paper lanterns in the trees to provide illumination as she stood and joined her friends nearby, grabbing a handful of berries from a plate along the way. Together they all journeyed to the Council, which was just gathering.

At the appearance of the Periodics Emeriti, a hush fell over the crowd, and the meeting began somewhat prematurely. The Periodics Emeriti immediately took control.

The situation was explained, including the various theories on the Tungsten-Wolfram alliance or overthrow. Everyone expressed outrage at Hydrogen's kidnapping, and several major undertakings were proposed to follow the wolframs and capture Tungsten and Wolfram. One Periodic in particular, a tiny horse with a brilliant "F" on her pale yellow side, was vociferous in her ire. She led her colorful Group-mates in calling for a prompt counterattack.

"We should set out *immediately* —" the tiny Periodic began.

"Lose no time!" interrupted a large, auburn Bromine who was standing beside her.

A bright yellow-green Chlorine chimed in, "If we focus our powers on Tungsten, we can overcome him —"

"Fluorine, Bromine, Chlorine," Kalium chided, "we mustn't get so excited...."

Julie stretched out her hand toward the smallest horse, who barely came to her chest. "You're so tiny!"

"Oh, rub it in!" exclaimed Fluorine in sarcastic response.

Julie looked up at Kalium, hurt. Kalium shook her head and breathed, "Fluorine is the smallest Periodic besides Hydrogen — although she's not the lightest — and for some reason she thinks that's a disadvantage. Don't antagonize her, please."

But Julie had no time to apologize to the bright-colored Periodic, who had flitted off and was again trumpeting the necessity of a rapid attack.

Aurum, having listened for over an hour to these grandiose plans, finally yawned, stood up on the raised platform in the huge Council glade, and cleared his throat. As if by magic, silence descended on the crowd. Julie was impressed.

"These plans are very nice," he began, "but they all put our dear Hydrogen in great danger. Don't you think, if they see an army coming after them, that the wolframs will hold Hydrogen hostage to stop that army from coming any closer? And when the army does come, won't they harm our little friend? No offense, Isotopes, about your size." Aurum nodded to the three Hydrogen Isotopes momentarily, then continued: "Wouldn't it be better if a small group sneaked up behind the wolframs, following their trail, and spirited Hydrogen away? Then, once she is safe, our army could move in." He paused, allowing the others to mull over his idea.

It didn't take very long for everyone to see the merits of Aurum's plan. He, Julie, the Isotopes, and the Chemy were immediately nominated to pursue the wolframs.

"I'm not going without Al," Julie asserted, and so Al the gebra was included.

"How about someone from Tungsten's family?" someone called out. "One of his Group-mates?"

"That's a good idea," Aurum stated. "Maybe you can talk some sense into him, if he's the root of the problem." He was looking down at a medium-sized, metallic gray horse standing on the ground at the edge of the platform.

"Come on up here, Chromium," Kalium suggested. "You and Molybdenum are probably our best sources of information about Tungsten."

Chromium nodded and mounted the platform by way of a wooden ramp set off to the side.

"Where is she, by the way?" Kalium continued.

"Molybdenum? She was too embarrassed to attend," Chromium replied, a shadow passing across his face. "Kalium, we've — we've received a lot of abuse because of what our Group-mate has done. I just don't understand why he went crazy. He was perfectly sane. And then one day he disappeared. Shortly thereafter, the wolframs began attacking anyone bearing wolframite ... and we got this note saying he was going to take over Mathematics.... It's so strange."

Kalium nodded in sympathy. The Chemy gave a low growl but made no further comment.

"Does anyone else know anything significant about Tungsten or Wolfram?" Argentum called.

There was a flicker off to the left, at the edge of the clearing. An immense, semi-transparent form drifted out of the woods, darkening the grass and trees behind it. Julie squinted at it and noted a vaguely equine shape. Was she seeing four legs? And a horse's head?

Nearly everyone in the clearing was watching the form. Into the oppressive silence, Argentum asked, "Do you have information?"

The cloud shifted from within, and two oblong red spots near the top closed momentarily, like eyes blinking. The cloud became more dense, taking on a more definite horse shape, but still said nothing. The newcomer towered over the Periodics in the glade, a giant, silent, Trojan-horse-like figure. Then, just as Argentum opened her mouth to repeat the question, a booming voice intoned: "THERE IS A HUMAN PRESENT." No emotion was apparent in the remark.

"Yes, so what?" Cuprum asked. He and Ferrum were eyeing the somber newcomer with mistrust.

"NO HUMAN MAY KNOW ME," the figure stated. Its mouth did not move, and Julie suddenly realized that she was hearing its voice *inside her head*.

"The situation calls for desperate measures," Hydrargyrum told it.

"Who is this guy?" Julie asked Kalium.

"It's a Periodic," Kalium answered. "I can tell you that much from its aura of power. But it must be a new one ... one the Humans haven't discovered yet. It must have a huge mass! And its atomic number ... higher than 112, easily. From its size, I would say it might even be a Group-mate of mine – of Potassium's, I mean. But I've never seen it before."

"I BEAR NEWS OF TUNGSTEN," the new Periodic intoned.

"What is it?" asked Argentum.

"HE IS NO LONGER IN MATHEMATICS. HE HAS RETREATED WITH HIS WOLFRAMS BACK INTO SCIENCE. THIS NEWS IS THREE DAYS OLD."

"In which direction is he going?" Kalium asked.

"BEARING APPROXIMATELY FORTY-FIVE DEGREES NORTH," the figure responded.

"Northeast of here," Natrium murmured. "Something tells me that's where the wolframs' trail will lead."

♀ ☾ ☉ ♂ ▽ ☿ ⊕

The next morning, Julie stood surveying her new traveling companions. They had gathered fodder and Human food, water, and a bag of odds and ends that was slung around Al's neck, hanging over one shoulder like a bookbag. Julie hoisted her own bookbag in the warm sunshine of the glade. Not long after delivering his tidings, the mysterious Periodic had filtered back through the woods, and Julie still wondered who he was.

The Periodics, both those who were going in pursuit of Hydrogen and those who were not, were quiet. Everyone seemed affected by the seriousness of the situation, concerned not only for the fate of their colleague, Hydrogen, but for that of Mathematics and Science as well. It seemed as if their very way of life was being affected by Tungsten's and/or Wolfram's rash behavior.

Julie tried not to worry. They were doing something about the problem, and that was thousands of times better than just sitting around. As she waited for the signal to depart, she thought about what might be happening in her own world. Had the hospitals found a new way to diagnose broken bones, since X-ray machines weren't working? Had people started using candles to light their homes? What about fluorescent lights? Did they use tungsten, too?

Suddenly the Chemy broke from the crowd and paced off through the forest, nose to the ground. Julie realized that he had begun tracking the wolframs' scent, and she followed him.

Deuterium, Tritium, and Protium, the Hydrogen Isotopes, along with Aurum, Chromium, Al, and several Periodics who weren't officially pursuing Hydrogen, trailed behind. The noise they made as they crashed through the underbrush troubled Julie, as she considered the possibility of another wolfram ambush ahead. Then she decided not to worry about it. The wolframs could probably smell them coming even if they tiptoed through the woods.

Aurum, beside her, seemed unusually alert. His deep gray eyes peered into the growth ahead with a concentration Julie had not seen before. He noticed her watching him and winked in her direction. She looked away, embarrassed to be caught staring.

One by one, the Periodics who were not part of the new group fell behind, forming a mass farther back. But the colorful Halogen Family, which included the outspoken Fluorine as well as Chlorine, Bromine, Iodine, and a quiet, evasive one named "At" — *Astatine*, Julie recalled — stayed close to them.

"Are you coming along?" Julie asked, making her voice sound merely curious. She wasn't sure how she felt about Fluorine and her Group-mates.

That stopped the Halogens for a moment.

"One of us should come along," Chlorine finally said, pawing the loam with a forehoof.

"Yes," agreed Bromine. "Hydrogen is, after all, considered part of our Family."

"What? I thought she was in the Alkali Family." Julie looked from the bright yellow Fluorine, past Bromine, to the dark Iodine standing nearby.

"No," Protium said, coming up behind her. "We Hydrogen Isotopes can gain an electron just as easily as we can lose one. Therefore, our electrical charge is considered to be negative one *and* positive one — get it? If we gain an electron, we have one more electron than we have protons, so the opposite charges don't balance anymore. Then the balance is negative one. If we gained two electrons, it would be negative two. If we lost two electrons — positive two."

Julie nodded. "I understand. It has to do with having more or fewer negative-charged electrons than positive-charged protons."

Protium seemed pleased. "Well, like I said, the Alkalis can be negative one *or* positive one because we can either gain or lose one electron. Mostly we lose it, of course, since big ions steal it to make eight, the most stable configuration. But here's where it gets tricky. The Halogens like to gain one electron. Know what that means? We're Halogens, too." Deuterium and Tritium nodded silently as she glanced at them.

"You are not!" objected Fluorine.

"We are too," chorused the Hydrogen isotopes.

"Technically," added Protium. Fluorine only scowled.

"How can you be negative one?" asked Julie as she resumed walking. The Halogens followed after her.

Deuterium responded, "It's as if there was an extra electron tacked on that comes off easily. Electrons have negative charges, remember?"

"Yes, I know that, but I've heard the Alkalis always lose their single outermost electron. Why should they gain one?"

"Usually we do lose one, but occasionally two are stable enough to sit around with. So we pick up one electron and just hold onto it, stable enough to sit there with only two."

"Oh."

Chromium had been listening to the discussion, and he now spoke up. "Yes, and different atoms have different numbers of electrons — and protons too, of course — so they can have larger or smaller negative charges. Some of my friends, like Carbon and Tin —"

"Or Stannum," Julie pointed out, quick to defend the former Periodics.

Chromium nodded, then continued, "— often have a negative four *and* a positive four charge, because there are four electrons in the outermost shell of electrons, just floating there ready to be taken."

"How can you be positive and negative at the same time?" Julie asked crossly, anxious over the Halogens' continued presence.

Chromium cocked his head. "Oh! Not at the same time. I mean, we can bond in either fashion."

"Okay, I get it. But I'm still not sure how you decide to gain or to lose electrons —"

"Well, it depends on how you look at it," Chromium explained patiently. "You see, all atoms like to have eight electrons — four pairs — in the outermost level, because that's the most stable configuration, like Protium said. So, in order to get eight there, the atoms of Carbon and Tin can either *lose* the outermost four, leaving the completed level just below them exposed, or *gain* four more to make eight in their own level. Do you see?"

Julie nodded.

Then Chromium kind of harrumphed. "The problem is, because four electrons are a lot to gain or lose, Carbon doesn't actually do that. Instead, the electrons get shared — that is, they form covalent bonds. I just used that example to make a point."

Bromine came up behind her, his dark red-brown body blending nicely with the tree trunks behind him. "So, anyway, that's why our charge is called 'positive one.' It's the same as saying 'negative seven,' because we have seven electrons in our outermost levels. But we're not likely to lose all seven of them; it's much easier to grab an electron from some atom nearby. So we're 'positive one' because we're going to take one in order to get eight."

"So 'positive' means how many electrons you're likely to grab and 'negative' means how many electrons you're likely to lose?" Julie wondered.

Bromine cocked his head. "I guess you could say that."

Aurum shot her an amused look, having overheard the last part of the discussion. "Are you learning about covalent bonding now?" he asked Julie. "We never had such a thing back in my day.... Oh, it existed, of course, but the Humans had no fancy names for it. They didn't know how atoms formed compounds."

"What's a covalent bond?" Julie inquired, looking at Bromine.

"That's where our atoms try to grab electrons from another

83

nonmetal, which holds onto them much better than a metal. Metal atoms let us steal electrons and keep them for ourselves. That forms an ionic bond, because both atoms become ions — atoms having an extra electron or two, or missing one or two. But other nonmetals, they're pretty tough. They make us share the electron with them — it revolves around both atoms, switching sometimes. Or something like that. So that's a covalent bond." Bromine cocked his head momentarily, his brow wrinkling with concentration. "It causes both atoms to stick together, what with the electrons flying around both of them like that. A molecule is formed — two atoms stuck together with electrical forces. Even though those forces are teeny-tiny, they're pretty strong."

"How big is an electron, anyway?" Julie asked.

"Teeny-tiny," Bromine repeated.

"No, really."

Bromine turned to Chlorine. "Do you know?"

Chlorine paused a moment for thought. "Its mass is ninety-one octillionths of a gram."

"WHAT??"

"In other words, ninety-one with twenty-seven zeroes in front of it," Fluorine replied absently, then: "Listen, guys, we can't all come along. Which one is going?"

The Halogens looked at each other. "Well," said Chlorine finally, sounding reluctant, "since you're getting along so well with the Human, Bromine, why don't you be our designated one to go?"

"Okay," Bromine replied instantly. He seemed to look forward to the prospect of a long journey, and took a deep breath with a smile on his face.

The other Halogens came to a stop and clustered behind them on the path. "Don't let them mess it up," Fluorine called, sounding disappointed, as they walked off through the trees.

"Why did they send you if they wanted to come?" Julie asked Bromine.

He looked down at her and shrugged. He was one heavy Periodic, Julie realized, but not very tall. Compared to the Hydrogen Isotopes, he was twice as tall, but only two-thirds the size of Aurum. Chromium, who was a couple of hands shorter than Aurum, also looked down upon the auburn-colored Periodic. Julie also noted that, although Chromium was taller, he was thinner than Bromine, indicating that his atoms had less atomic weight.

Then Julie looked at Aurum's portly figure and didn't even wonder how massive his atoms must be. She giggled and climbed up on Al's back, using the shoulder bag for support. She slid her leg under its weight and it bounced against her as Al cantered through the woods.

$$♀ ☾ ♂ ▽ ☿ ⊕$$

They stopped that night at the edge of the Elemental Forest. Julie, gazing out at the star-bleached plain, shook her head. "Science looks just like Mathematics!" she exclaimed.

"Well, they *are* similar," Al told her, turning his head slightly. "You use math in your science classes at school, don't you?"

"Yes," Julie responded.

"And your math classes use scientific examples for word problems, don't they?"

"Often," she admitted.

"Well, there you go. The two are intricately related. By the way, a lot of the axioms and properties you use in math class were derived by scientific experiments and observations." Al settled to the ground, and when Julie hopped off his back, she saw the contented expression on his face.

"What's for dinner, Al?" she inquired.

Al looked at her, then stared pointedly at the grass around his feet. She laughed at the old joke, remembered from her last visit, then asked, "No, really?"

Al fumbled at the catch to his bag with his lips, then withdrew a sack of small cubes. Peering through the plastic, Julie saw in the dim light that, unlike the cubed food she had sampled earlier in Mathematics, which started out white, these cubes were pink.

"Is this cubed food?" she inquired uncertainly.

"In a manner of speaking," Al told her, handing her — or *mouthing, rather,* she thought — a waterbag.

Setting one cube down on the resealed plastic bag, Julie dribbled a little water onto two cubes, expecting them to expand into some sort of foodstuff. Instead, the pink cubes shimmered — and *eight* white cubes popped into being.

"What is this?!" she exclaimed.

"Cubed cubed food," Al explained, looking smug.

"How did that happen?" Julie asked.

"By accident, at first, I imagine." Al sniffed at the new cubes. "Put the rest back and expand two. I'm hungry."

"You have grass!"

"Yes, but I'd rather have peanut butter," he replied.

"How can you tell it's peanut butter?" Julie wondered out loud. Following his directions, she saw that, indeed, it was — eight peanut-butter sandwiches now existed where two white cubes had just been.

"Its smell," Al replied. "Let me have one, please."

♀ ☾ ♂ ▽ ☿ ⊕

They divided the night into five watch-shifts, with two to a shift and the Chemy, by himself, as the first shift. As Julie rolled herself into the thick green blanket Al had been wearing on his back, she gazed up at the stars, wondering what elements were in them.

"Al," she asked, "what Periodics control the stars?"

Al looked up at the white-pocked sky. "I don't know," he replied, then tucked his legs under him, stretched out his neck on the ground, and closed his eyes. "Protium, Deuterium, Tritium, do you know?"

The three Isotopes, who were closest, shook their heads sleepily.

"The stars are made of plasma," Protium reminded her after a moment. "Plasma isn't really made of normal atoms, but atoms that have lost all their electrons. Atoms that have been changed into ions."

"But their nuclei are still the same," Julie insisted.

"Yes, but the nuclei are constantly changing," Protium told her. "Fusion happens in plasma, so not even the nuclei keep the same number of protons and neutrons for long. In fusion, two nuclei become one, forming an atom twice as big."

Julie thought about that.

"... However," Protium added, sounding on the verge of sleep, "most of the nuclei are technically hydrogen and helium nuclei, because they have only one or two protons. But heavier elements are said to exist there. I don't know. I've never been in the plasma state myself. Maybe Hydrogen...." He drifted off, leaving Julie alone with her thoughts. After a moment, they, too, faded into the darkness and she slept.

Julie's watch that night was with Al, and she tried to reinitiate the conversation they had begun before going to sleep. "What do you know about plasma, Al?"

"Only that it is one of the States of Matter," Al replied.

"And where are those States?" Julie inquired, knowing that they were physical regions somewhere in Science.

Al's ears perked forward. "Somewhere in the direction we're headed, actually," he said. "I wonder...."

He paused so long, lost in his own thoughts, that Julie prompted him, "What?"

"I wonder if that's where Tungsten is." Al sat gazing up at the stars, shifting his weight from time to time. "I'm trying to figure out if there's anywhere he could hide in there."

"What are the States of Matter like?"

"Well, because you're a Human and I'm not a Periodic, we won't experience their full effects. But the power of those regions is so strong that any Periodics or Isotopes that go into the States come under their influence."

"And what happens?" Julie absently dug into the earth with a short stick she had found nearby.

"Well, first of all, their boiling and melting points define which State they have to enter first."

"What?" Julie looked up, blinking.

"If they're liquid at room temperature, they have to enter the Liquid State first. If they're solid, they enter Solid first." Al reached his nose down to the ground to munch some grass growing there. "So that means our group is going to split up."

"That's not good!" Julie exclaimed. "Where are we going to meet again?"

Al considered while Julie noticed the trench she was digging in the ground. Then she stared at the stick, wondering where it had come from. The half-dead leaves still clinging to the bark were square and looked vaguely familiar — down to the tiny "E,"

"A," "F," and "W" inscribed in the corners — but no trees having those leaves grew nearby. "Where did I get this stick?" she asked, interrupting Al's thoughts.

Al glanced at it, then nibbled delicately on its end. "It tastes like Chemistree. You probably picked it up somewhere in the Forest. Rolled up in the blanket or something. Now, as for rejoining...." Al cocked his head. "Maybe we'll meet inside Gas or something. Maybe we won't have to go in at all. We'll just see where the wolframs lead us."

Julie plucked off the leaves and let them drift to the ground. She faced away from Al, looking out over the dark terrain.

The rest of their shift was spent in watchful silence as they gazed across their nearly featureless surroundings. When the correct amount of time had passed, marked by the drifting stars, they woke Deuterium and Tritium for the next shift and went back to sleep.

♀ ☾ ♂ ▽ ☿ ⊕

Julie awoke shivering as chill winds blew over the plain, tossing the grass before them into dancing waves and the trees behind them into convulsive gesturing with a multitude of limbs. Dark clouds scudded across the sky, alternately dimming and brightening the piercing yellow light. Julie squinted and sat up, feeling at her tangled hair and picking grass out of her blanket.

"What time is it?" she groaned.

"Just after sunup," Chromium informed her. Somewhat hesitantly, he crossed to her and helped her pick grass out of the blanket, using his teeth. She patted his thick mane, rubbed behind his ears, and stood up, stretching and groaning again. There was just something about sleeping on hard, cold ground that did not agree with her.

Julie took a few steps and went to lean against Bromine, but jumped back, alarmed, as she sank several inches into him. Even as she moved, she realized that Bromine's natural state must be a liquid.

She poked gently at him. There was resistance, but not as much as if she had leaned against a wall, and she noticed a viscous sort of flowing as Bromine's side regained its former shape. The same thing had occurred when she first went to touch Francium, who was also a liquid, during her first visit to Mathematics. Bromine chuckled, noting her surprise.

That reminded Julie of a question that had been pestering her for a while. She went to Tritium, who nuzzled her, and asked, "How come you guys are solid? I thought your natural state was a gas."

"Oh, it is," Tritium told her, shaking his head and causing hair to drift off in the wind. "But we make an effort to be solid when you're around."

"Do you normally have that much control over your states?"

"Yes. It's very easy." To demonstrate, Tritium concentrated for a moment, then became liquid underneath Julie's hand. She jerked back from the strange sensation. "It's just that our element has to be really, really cold before it becomes a liquid," Tritium explained.

"Then why, when we reach the States of Matter, *if* we reach the States of Matter, don't you all concentrate on being solid, and we can walk into the Solid State without splitting up?"

The others paused, and Julie realized that this was their first cognizance that they were headed toward the States of Matter.

"It wouldn't work," Chromium said finally. "Entrance to the States goes by our state at room temperature. Period. Concentrating on being in a particular state wouldn't help. We have to enter at our room temperature states. It's one of the rules of the region."

"Why?"

"I don't know. There's no scientific reason," Chromium answered. "It just is. Maybe it's because we're headed out of nature when we enter the States, in a general sort of symbolic way, so it goes by our states in nature. I don't know."

Julie, shivering, dug through her bookbag and encountered her jacket balled near the top. She donned it, grateful for her meager planning. Then, as an afterthought, she fastened her watch around her wrist. She didn't remember taking it off, but she wasn't surprised; so much had happened since arriving in Science that she had barely remembered to eat.

"What's that?" Al inquired, thrusting his nose near Julie's wrist.

"A watch."

"What does it watch?"

"It tells me what time it is."

"What does it say now?"

Julie grimaced at the circular face. "It says 7:10. And that's too early."

"It lies?"

Julie looked up in surprise. "No, no. It's telling the truth. I just think that's too early to be awake."

"Oh."

Julie ate the rest of the stale sandwiches from last night, then spread the blanket over Al's back, helped him with the shoulder bag, and climbed on. Al enjoyed carrying her so much that she knew he would raise a fit if she were to ride anyone else, so she didn't even propose the idea.

$$\venus \moon \mars \triangledown \mercury \earth$$

They rode across the windy landscape for hours, pausing for lunch, then continued until sunset. Over the course of the day, Julie saw nothing but waving grass and foliage, including small bushes. Some of the trees they passed at first were marked as "Chemistrees," but as they got deeper into Science, the trees grew more specialized, and Julie began to see such species as "Biochemistrees," "Geochemistrees," and "Electrochemistrees." As night closed upon them, they paused in a small cluster of the latter and made camp.

"Al," she asked, as she fiddled with the bag of cubes for dinner, "what would happen if I uncubed just one cube? Not the double-cubed ones, just the ordinary white kind."

"You'd get one large sandwich," Al replied instantly.

"Why?"

"Because one cubed is one. Period. One to the fifteenth power is one. To the twentieth power. To the hundred and seventh power. Always."

"Okay, then, what would happen if I uncubed three at the same time?"

"You'd get twenty-seven little sandwiches."

"… Because three cubed is three times three times three, or twenty-seven," Julie finished. "But why small?"

"Because, although numbers are endless, the amount of matter that the cube contains is fixed."

Julie puzzled over this for a few moments. "Because I'm dividing the stuff each time?"

Al cocked his head. "Um, no. Okay, here's an explanation. It has to do with the way the cubes are made. You take one apple, say, and combine it with another apple, then another apple, and by some complicated process you get the little white cubes you're used to. So there's the matter from three apples incorporated into one cube, which, when uncubed, produces one large apple with the substance from three apples in it. Now, you do the same thing again — multiply three apples together. Now you have another cube, just like the first. Now you uncube that one along with your first cube. By definition, eight apples must be produced, because two cubed equals eight, but there's only the matter from six apples incorporated into the two cubes. You begin to see? Take three more apples and make another cube, then uncube all three together ... twenty-seven apples have to be produced, but there's only enough matter to make nine normal apples, so the apples produced are really small. That's why I tell you to uncube two at a time. It's about the right amount of stuff, and it's not too shrunk. Understand?"

Julie nodded wordlessly. She had no idea it was that complicated!

As she lay beneath the trees that night, she thought she saw tiny blue flashes above her head. Sitting up and peering into the growth, she was sure of it.

"Lightning?" she asked aloud, and Aurum stirred beside her.

"No," he sighed, "that's one of those newfangled electro-chemistrees."

From the way he said it, Julie was sure that the tree was not new. "New" to a Periodic Emeritus could be anything since the Dark Ages.

"What makes it do that?" she asked.

"It's the transferal of electrons," Chromium answered, sounding tired. "Copper and platinum and salt bridges and things. It seems that, when one element gives up electrons more easily than another element, the second element takes them."

"Like a covalent bond," Julie suggested, recalling the term.

"No, no. That happens in space. This transferal occurs in some kind of solution — water, with salts dissolved in it. And it's not really a bond."

Julie looked up at the tree. "It doesn't look like it has water up there."

"It has to. It's an electrochemistree. That's what they're all about." Aurum sniffed at the tree, settled deeper into the grass, and began snoring. Julie followed soon after, but without the buzz-saw effect.

The next morning, she was as stiff as ever. Her watch the previous night with Al was, as before, uneventful, and she fell asleep right after it was over, but it wasn't a restful sleep.

"Ow, Al!" she exclaimed, after the gebra woke her up and bid her a "jubilant morning." "I'm sore!"

Al cocked his head, looking troubled. "Perhaps you are sleeping wrong," he stated.

Julie sat up and sighted the Chemy lying close by, on the other side of the electrochemistree. He was staring up into its depths.

"What do you see, Chemy?" she asked, stretching.

The beast flicked his tail, and his emerald gaze swept down to encompass her. "The miniature lightning," he replied, "is not something most alchemists employed to effect the Philosopher's Stone." Then he went back to looking at the tree. "But...." He said nothing more and didn't seem as if he had any intention of doing so.

"Whatever," said Deuterium after a few moments.

♀ ☾ ♂ ▽ ☿ ⊕

They rode once more across the plain, the Chemy leading the way, nose sometimes to the ground, sometimes lifted to the air. Julie realized that she had not noticed him very much in the past couple of days. As he trotted along, she knew why: He blended perfectly with his surroundings. Always difficult to discern because of his unique coloration — *or lack thereof,* she added — his very texture merged into the long grasses. If she hadn't already known he was there, she wasn't certain she would have seen him at all. Watching the Chemy, she understood how lions hunted so well on the savanna, back on her world. No one could see them coming.

"There it is!" Deuterium exclaimed.

"What?" Julie's head jerked up and she sighted a row of dark blots on the horizon.

"That is the Solid State," Bromine answered her.

"You were right, Julie," Protium told her. "The wolframs are leading us there."

"That must be where Tungsten and Wolfram are hiding," Chromium stated.

"With Hydrogen," Tritium added.

They broke into a gallop and the dark blots soon resolved into stubby points, then roughly triangular mountains. The Iso-topes pulled up after a time, tired, and the rest of the group came to a halt. Julie jumped down from Al's back and stood craning her neck for a better look.

"How tall are the mountains?" she asked.

"Not very tall," Al told her, "as mountains go. They conceal the rest of the States and mark the outer boundary."

"The boundary around them all?" Julie turned to Al, surprised.

"Yes." Al nodded.

Chromium perked his ears toward her. "Solid surrounds Liquid, which surrounds Gas, which surrounds Plasma," he informed her. "It's pretty interesting. You'll see."

Julie rolled her eyes. She'd heard that before!

After lunch, they drank from a trickling stream and started off again at a leisurely pace. The Chemy, as always, led the way, his tufted tail swaying like a cattail bent sharply in the breeze. As they cantered, Julie balanced herself, unslung her bookbag from her shoulder, and rummaged through it. She drew out her forgotten soda, took a sip, then grimaced. "It's flat!"

Aurum looked over at her. "All the carbonic acid has decomposed into carbon dioxide and water. I told you that would happen," he said solemnly, but with a twinkle in his eye. "Now the evolved carbon dioxide has escaped as gas."

"It demonstrates change," the Chemy rumbled back toward her. "Liquid evolves to gas, gas escapes, and the substance is changed in character."

"Right. But of course that's a *chemical* change, not just a physical one, because the acid became carbon dioxide."

The Chemy nodded. Julie suspected that he was trying to teach her something, but she had no clue what that might be. She caught herself looking around for a trash can to put the soda in, sighed, and put it back in her bag. She'd have to recycle it later; there were no bins here.

$$♀ ☾ ♂ ▽ ☿ ⊕$$

They traversed the wide plain all day, and when night spread across its green expanse, they were almost at the foot of the mountains. Here the ground was slightly hilly, as if looking forward to its ascension into mighty peaks.

Gazing toward Solid, Julie saw that the hills grew more pronounced until naked rock thrust through the greenery toward the sky. None of the peaks looked high enough to hold snow, but between two ridges, she thought she saw the last light of day blaze ice into salmon-aquamarine brilliance.

6
The Solid State

As the morning sun rose, long black shadows stretched behind the peaks of Solid to the left. After a brief breakfast, the group set off across the hills. They were impatient now, fed by the knowledge that they were close and by the danger that Tungsten and Wolfram posed.

They crossed the foothills carefully and, as the humps grew more precipitous, wove their way along stream beds between the mounds. There was no sign of the wolframs, but caution came to them without thought. At last the foothills arched upward into stone, spewing out a narrow trail of gravel between two vertical peaks.

Julie looked at the path with some trepidation. "I guess this is where we part."

"Yes," agreed Deuterium. "The second we place hoof upon that path, we'll be transferred to the Gas State."

"And I to the Liquid State," Bromine said.

Aurum looked around. "Well, never fear, Human," he stated, "I'll stay with you." Chromium nodded in agreement.

"Let's agree to meet," Protium said. "We'll wait at the very edge of Gas. You, Bromine, wait at the edge of Liquid nearest to Solid, on the path." Bromine gave a nod.

Then each took a deep breath and, one by one, stepped onto the gravel trail. As the Isotopes did so, they disappeared, as did Bromine. At last only Julie, Al, Chromium, Aurum, and the Chemy were left.

As Julie passed the threshold, she felt a very gentle tingling. The land opened up behind the row of mountains, and she saw a half-crescent of mountains extending forward to either side for miles and miles.

Julie caught her breath, seeing the rough, rocky terrain on both sides of the path. Compared to the mountains, it was flat, but not much. Gravel beds led down to brightly-hued and darker stone, some containing sparkling gems. Frozen pools of water lay beside the path in places, and other frozen substances Julie didn't recognize lay beyond.

The Chemy gave a satisfied rumble as he lifted his muzzle into the breeze. It was cold here, and the breeze was strong enough to flutter Julie's hair about her face. Deciding to braid it back, she delved into her bookbag, searching for a hair tie, but came up with only her soda bottle. She brought it out in mere reflex, started to put it back, then stopped and examined it.

"Al," she said, "the soda is frozen."

Al peered into the bottle. "It sure is."

Chromium glanced down at her. "Well, this *is* the Solid State," he said. "Everything that enters is immediately changed into its solid form. Like that radon over there." His muzzle pointed to a peculiar gray-white rock formation behind a translucent vertical sheet of ice. Julie couldn't be sure of what she saw, for the ice nearly concealed it.

"I wouldn't advise that you get too near the radon," Chromium told her. "It's radioactive."

"What about the ice in front of it?" she asked, returning the bottle and drawing out her jacket. "Is it water?"

"Yes," Aurum replied before Chromium could answer. Chromium threw him a dissatisfied look.

Julie peered as far down the path as she could, but there were many dips and bends that obscured its length.

"Let's get moving," Aurum suggested. They looked ahead to find the Chemy ranging some distance down the path, nose still in the air, smiling with some ambiguous joy.

"You really like the States of Matter, don't you?" Julie asked him as they caught up.

The Chemy gazed tranquilly at her. "Alchemy involves several changes of state before the Quintessence may be evolved."

"The Quintessence?"

"The Philosopher's-Stone-type-of-thing," Aurum murmured to her. "The perfection he's always talking about."

"I thought gold was made!"

"Here we go again," Aurum muttered.

"Perfection," the Chemy corrected her. "Not simply gold. Correct balance of the four Elements achieves the Quintessence."

They were making good time, and rock walls towered steeply on either side of this part of the path, so Julie was willing to explore this subject now that there was nothing to look at but stone. "What elements? You mean like hydrogen, helium, lithium —"

"Earth, Water, Air, and Fire."

Julie looked at Aurum, waiting for an explanation she knew the Chemy wouldn't give.

"According to the ancient Greeks," the golden Periodic obliged her, "those four elements made up everything. Later, the more specific elements were discovered."

"The Elements," the Chemy persisted, "correspond to the States of Matter, do they not?"

Julie gave that some thought. "Solid, Earth; Liquid, Water; Gas, Air ... Plasma, Fire?"

"Exactly." The Chemy nodded solemnly and his smile widened. "There is reason such a parallel can be made."

"What is that reason?"

"The two systems are compatible, for they grew from each other."

"What systems?" Julie was lost.

"Alchemy and its modern outgrowths."

"Chemistry, you mean?"

The Chemy nodded again, and his smile opened enough to give Julie a glimpse of the dagger-like fangs.

"And how is this going to help us?" Julie asked.

The Chemy paused for a moment and faced Julie. She shivered as his eyes rippled like mercury pools reflecting emerald light. "That, Human, is for you to discover." He turned and resumed pacing across the gravel.

Julie was speechless for a moment. "Wait a moment!" she exclaimed. "I don't know what you're talking about."

The Chemy did not reply.

"You expect me to do something about Tungsten? Using *alchemy*?"

The Chemy shook his mane. "Using chemistry. One shall supply the alchemy."

Julie was struck speechless again. *He will supply the alchemy!* she thought sardonically. *As if I know enough about chemistry to...!* "You can't be serious!"

The look the Chemy shot her in response seemed serious.

They trudged across the gravel for nearly an hour while the path swerved, dipped, and rose. After a while, Julie got back on Al, but the chill wind still took its toll. She was shivering and weary as they followed the path, and soon she lost interest in her surroundings.

Then a signpost caught her eye. Made of bronze or some other dull yellow metal, it depicted an eagle with outstretched wings and a triangular symbol clutched in its talons. The triangle was pointed downward, and what looked like a horizontal capital "I" stretched across it.

"What does that mean?" Julie asked, pointing up at it.

The Chemy took one glance and replied, "Earth."

"Is that what the triangular symbol stands for?"

"Yes."

"What about the eagle?"

"Earth."

"They both mean Earth?"

"Yes."

"Why?"

"… This path is called Earth," Aurum answered, as the Chemy did not seem willing to.

Suddenly the path delved between two high walls, as it had before, but halfway through the canyon they found that a rock slide had blocked their further progress.

"Of all the luck!" Chromium exclaimed.

The rock slide brought a complete end to the path, as it was nearly a hundred feet in height and stretched from wall to wall.

"What should we do now?" Al mused.

The Chemy turned toward them. "The Sun must seek Air. The Colorful One must seek Fire. The Human and her numerical companion must stay with one. Caution."

They backtracked out of the canyon, and to her surprise, Aurum and Chromium took off across the landscape to the right of the path, while the Chemy led her and Al down the gravel bed to the left.

"What's going on, Al?" Julie asked her friend.

"As near as I can tell," the gebra replied, "the Chemy just sent Aurum and Chromium to look for two other paths. I have no idea where we're going."

"To Water," the Chemy responded.

"These are all paths in Solid?" Julie inquired.

"In the States, yes."

Julie assumed he meant that the paths traveled all the way through the States, not just through Solid. She sighed, wondering how long this journey was going to last.

$$ \female \quad \moon \quad \male \quad \triangledown \quad \mercury \quad \earth $$

As they walked, Julie noticed that the Chemy kept looking around them, sometimes growling under his breath.

"What's the matter?" she asked, shivering, as they paused for lunch. Julie was glad she had leftover uncubed food, because all of their water was solid. *Even if this wasn't Solid,* she thought, *the water would be solid because it's so cold!*

"One scents wolframs," the Chemy informed her, and a new chill washed over her. "One scented them on Earth as well. That is why we journey to Water."

Just as they began again, there came a loud clatter to their right, as of hard hooves against stone, and a large ram appeared. His immense horns curved back over his long, skinny ears, and his thick coat blended perfectly with the white frozen mass of hydrogen — Julie had asked about it at lunch — behind him. As they looked up, at least twenty more rams appeared behind him.

"This is bad news," Al prophesied.

The ram let out a challenging bleat, and suddenly the entire group was clacking across the frozen hydrogen and stone toward them.

The Chemy leapt in front of Julie, crouching low to the ground and snarling. The rams shimmered ... and transformed into wolframs.

Their savage, fang-baring grimaces sent spears of icy terror into Julie's chest, but she struggled to get a hold on herself, forced in a deep breath, and clutched at Al's stiff mane. The gebra was watching the wolframs with apprehension, half-blocking Julie with his body.

The Chemy's flying claws gave pause to the front ranks of the ferocious beasts, and Julie had time to fumble for her pocket-knife, a relic from home she had rediscovered while rummaging through her bookbag the day before. *It isn't much,* she thought, *but it's something.*

Al reared and stomped viciously, and a wolfram jumped backward from his strike, still snarling in defiance. It dodged in and out again, trying to lure Al forward, but Al wasn't going to budge from the side of his Human friend. Julie, backed up against his side, watched the Chemy slash out at the encroaching wolframs. He paused for a moment, and Julie feared he was weakening. Then, without warning, the rock beneath the wolframs' paws buckled, began to glow a bright cherry red, and sagged inward. The wolframs sank into the forming liquid — lava, Julie noted — without being harmed by its fiery temperature, but they became understandably nonplused when the lava hardened abruptly around their legs.

"How did you do that?" Julie demanded, breathless with awe.

"Heat," replied the Chemy, throwing her a smug glance.

Al was smiling broadly. "That's a wonderful trick, Chemy!" The beast had taken time out to lick his somewhat invisible fur into place.

♀ ☾ ♂ ▽ ☿ ⊕

They traveled onward across Solid, leaving the entrapped wolframs behind. As the sun was beginning to set behind them to the left, they came to another gravel path. Beside this one was another signpost, this time of an angel with widespread wings, holding up another triangle. This triangle also pointed downward but lacked the horizontal "I" of the previous one.

"What does this say?" Julie asked the Chemy.

"Water," he replied.

The turned to travel down the new path, and Julie asked why they needed to use the paths at all.

"The regions' barriers are impassable except by means of the paths," Al answered her. "I know a little about this place, though not much. I've just heard you have to use the paths."

Not long after the wolframs' frustrated yelping had faded into the distance, it reappeared and began to increase in volume.

"They couldn't have gotten free," Al grumbled. "It must be another pack."

The Chemy pointed his ears in the direction of the racket, then pressed them flat against his head.

"Pursuit," he growled. "The Human must hide." He looked around, sighted a small cave to one side of the path, and stalked into it, his nose twitching. Soon he reemerged, looked into Al's eyes for a moment, then glanced at the opening in the dark basalt. Al, reading his unspoken message, entered the cave, bearing Julie on his back.

"What are you going to do, Chemy?" Julie inquired, as the Chemy-lion nodded gravely to her and trotted away.

"Wolframs may not chase that which they do not see," the Chemy's voice floated back to them. "However, they will chase that which they do see. Remain in obscurity until the sun disappears."

"I think he means sunset," Al told her. "He's going to lead a diversion."

Julie sighed, wrapping her arms around her for warmth. "I guess the smoke from a fire would give us away, wouldn't it?" She dismounted and explored the cave, which was really little more than a shallow opening in the ground. In the center was a small, circular blackened area, and a scrap of fabric was lying against one wall. Someone had used the cave before, but from the decomposed state of the rag, not for a long time.

"It probably would," Al agreed, "if you could even start a fire. This is Solid, after all. Fire isn't solid."

"What is fire?"

Al was stumped by that one. "Gas?" he suggested.

"Heat," sighed Julie. She huddled against one wall, shivering. After a moment's thought, Al exited and reentered the cave a moment later, carrying a black rock in his mouth. He repeated the process several times, and soon there was a small pile of the stones — coal — in the center of the cave, on top of the circle.

"Maybe a little fire wouldn't hurt," he explained. "You're a Human; see if you can start one."

Julie shrugged. She had seen the Chemy start a fire in a much more unlikely situation than this.

"We need some way to make a spark," she said.

"What about banging two rocks together?" Al proposed. "I've seen that done once."

"Me, too. But what rocks were they?" Julie sat and thought for a while. "I'm pretty sure if you bang steel against something, it will spark. Steel against what? ... Flint. It was flint, Al. Go find some flint."

"What does it look like?"

"I don't know. We don't have a lot of time," Julie worried. "Maybe there's some around here." She wandered into the rear area of the cave, where the ceiling swooped down toward the floor. There was something jammed into the angle where they met.

She reached in cautiously and felt rough fabric. Drawing it out, she saw that it was a hard bundle of objects wrapped in burlap. Whoever had been here before had left supplies behind. Julie carefully unwrapped the burlap and saw two medium-sized, rough-edged stones. One felt smooth like glass, yet was sharp along the edges. In addition, there were two cubes of cubed food, a water canteen filled with ice, and some small, round, metal disks Julie assumed were coins.

"I think this might be flint," she thought aloud, fingering the smooth stone. She brought it toward the coal and struck her pocket-knife hard against it.

"Be careful," Al advised.

"I am." She tried again, as hard as she could, and thought she saw a faint yellow flash in the dimness of the cave. "Al, bring me that rag, please."

Al looked around until he sighted the rag, then kicked it toward her, unwilling to put it in his mouth. Julie caught it and placed it on the floor beneath where she was experimenting with the stone. She struck again, but nothing happened. On her fourth try, she saw another tiny flash.

"This is working, Al!" she exclaimed. Concentrating then, she took a deep breath. *Please work*, she commanded silently, shivering. *Think, Julie*, she coached herself, *think about how warm it's going to be with a fire. Think about the fire. A fire would create heat, which would burn this coal by uniting its carbon with oxygen in the air. It's called oxidation. That would make carbon dioxide, but there would also be heat. If only I can make a spark!* Concentrating as hard as she could on the chemical process, she struck — and a brilliant spark flew down to the rag, igniting it.

"I did it, Al!" she shouted, then remembered that they were supposed to be in hiding. She moved the rapidly disappearing rag onto the coal, and the fire sank low as it used up its easy fuel. "Ignite the coal, please," she whispered aloud. "Oxidize that carbon!" She envisioned the little carbon atoms joining with two oxygens each, forming carbon dioxide gas, which floated away.

With a stubborn flicker, the coal beneath the rag burst into blue flame.

Al smiled and sank down beside the fire. "Thank goodness!"

he sighed. "Your Human powers are very useful, Julie."

"You think I used Human powers?" she asked, dubious.

"You must have. Only a Human could make fire in Solid. Fire isn't solid, so normally it couldn't exist here. But you made it." He closed his eyes, still smiling, enjoying the warmth. "Besides, I heard you muttering about oxidation right before the coal ignited. Because you knew the chemical process, you could make it happen. That's impressive."

"I guess it is." Julie sank back, still not certain. Could her Human powers finally have started working? Maybe the Chemy had known, and that's why he had told her she could use chemistry against Tungsten. But did she really have a chance?

7
The Liquid State

THE SUNSET brought greater chill, coupled with the fact that the fire had nearly died. Julie shivered in her jacket, pressed next to Al's blanketed side.

"When we walk, we'll be warmer," Al told her. "Let's go. It's sunset."

They emerged from the cave, looking out over the darkening landscape with dread. Julie left behind the objects wrapped in burlap, thinking that their owner might return. Besides, she didn't need the supplies, and the owner might.

They followed the path called Water beyond the cave into another gully, where they discovered another rock slide blocking their progress. They backtracked and exited the path just before it went into the gully, but found that the ground dipped into fearsome valleys on either side. There was no way around, unless they traveled all the way around the valleys, one way or the other, and then they might as well just seek out another path and take that instead.

"I know the wolframs did this," she glowered. "They're trying to keep us from Tungsten."

"They're doing a good job, too," Al noted.

They decided to try to find the path called Air or Fire, whichever came next, so they took off once more cross-country, weaving their way around awesome rock formations and frozen elements. Sometimes, where centuries had laid a thin veneer of dirt upon the rock, they saw impressions of four-toed, clawed paws or tiny cloven hooves, and sometimes the two mixed together.

"The wolframs have been all over this place," Julie observed. "I wonder how long Tungsten's been here."

"Probably quite a while," Al opined. "It must have taken a long time to block off the Earth and Water paths."

"Then the other two paths are probably blocked off as well."

"I hope not."

On top of the smaller, four-toed prints, there suddenly appeared a single line of huge, five-toed ones.

"The Chemy!" Julie exclaimed.

"How do you know?"

"I've seen his prints before. Look!" She ran forward to where a dark splotch appeared on a white bed of frozen hydrogen. "He's coloring his prints! He did that before, too! They turn black, then starry...." Julie struggled to remember what came next. "He must want us to follow him."

"That's fine with me," Al agreed. "Let's hurry."

$$♀ ☾ ♂ ▽ ☿ ⊕$$

The sun sank over the stark wasteland, and Julie continued to shiver, huddled against Al for warmth. They were stooping now to make out the black prints against rock or ice, straining their eyes in the gathering darkness. Just as the night took over, Julie peered ahead and saw tiny white spots on the ground ahead. She hurried forward and stared at them. They were grouped in rough circles, looking like miniature stars enclosed in a patch of gray.

"His second color!" Julie exclaimed. "Thank goodness the white glows in the dark!"

The luminous speckles led them over hill and down, around massive piles of frozen something-or-other, across narrow strips of black rock over awe-inspiring chasms, until they came at last to another gravel pathway.

"This must be either Fire or Air!" Julie cried. They followed it — the paw prints did also — and soon came to a signpost that depicted a lion bearing an upward-pointing triangle on its back. Across the triangle was a horizontal line with a little upward-jabbing serif on the right side.

"I wonder which it is," Al contemplated.

"I don't know."

They followed the path until a second row of mountains came into view. Gradually the mountains grew larger, but the farther they went, the more tired Julie became. She had gotten some sleep in the cave, but not enough, and it was now late into the night.

"Al, can we stop?"

"I don't think we should."

It wasn't much later that, as they rounded a bend, the Chemy reappeared.

"One may not stay too long," he told them without preamble. "Danger still lurks nearby. The Human should rest here until light returns."

They looked where the beast indicated and found another cave, smaller but serviceable.

"One will continue to lead the Human inward," the Chemy resumed as they explored their new shelter. "However, the Human must use her abilities in Liquid to prevent her belongings from melting."

Julie was shocked. The idea had never occurred to her. "How do you know I'll be able to do that?"

"The Human can."

"But how do you know?"

"The Human has survived here and not frozen."

"So?"

In the faint light cast by the real stars high above, the Chemy looked annoyed. "Frozen hydrogen, while not at absolute zero, is near."

"So?" Julie still didn't see the point, but Al gasped.

"You mean some of these frozen hydrogen beds we've been walking on have been at almost zero degrees Kelvin — *negative* two hundred and seventy-five degrees Celsius?" Al exclaimed.

The Chemy nodded.

Al looked flabbergasted, and so did Julie, as the realization sank in.

"How come I haven't frozen?" Al wanted to know.

"The Human is your companion. Her ... ambiance extends over you."

Al shook his head rapidly.

"Chemy," Julie said, "I started a fire."

The Chemy looked proud of her. "One is pleased. Human abilities, while innate, are for the most part latent. It is difficult to use them consciously."

The Chemy nudged her hand with his head, turned, and bounded away. Star-sprinkled prints glowed in his wake.

Afterward, Julie spent half an hour trying to heat up her

"ambiance" so she wasn't so cold, but that didn't seem to make much difference. It kept her alive but not warm. Finally she cuddled up next to Al and fell asleep, shivering slightly, but not just with cold.

The morning sun woke them, streaming into their little shelter like liquid fire. Julie and Al had eaten the last of the uncubed food the day before, so they had nothing to eat this morning — unless they wanted to try the remaining cubes without water, which might be awkward if they uncubed themselves in their stomachs.

"Oh, well," she mused, "we're headed into Liquid next. I'm sure there'll be plenty of water."

They crawled out of the cave and set out once more toward the mountains that now loomed close, casting their shadows off to the right.

"That's the boundary, isn't it?" Julie asked, and Al nodded.

They arrived at the mountains before midday and climbed the gravel path that clawed its way up between two. At the top, they paused, and Julie gasped at the panorama before her.

Stretching for miles, as if in a gigantic bowl formed by the second ring of mountains, was a vast sheet of multi-hued liquids. Broad pools of deep blue alternated with patches of bright red, brilliant white, yellow, gray, brown, and green. Everywhere Julie looked was another shade, all liquid, all flowing together.

The gravel path disappeared. In its place was a ribbon of mercury, like a long bubble of mirror on top of the swirling surface. As Julie followed it with her eyes, she could make out a deep gray cloud on the horizon, hovering near the surface of the liquid.

"Um, Al ... ," she began.

"Yes?"

"How are we going to walk on mercury?"

"Don't ask me," Al replied. "You're the Human."

"Great."

Julie paused for several minutes, trying to figure out how she was going to keep all her clothes and belongings solid in a region so manifestly given to liquid. It was probably the same way she was going to walk on liquid mercury. She had to keep an "ambiance" about her of solidness.

A warm breeze blew off the currents below. It was not as cold in Liquid as in Solid. At least that was a mercy.

She took a deep breath, trying to decide how to go about creating this mysterious "ambiance." She couldn't believe she was doing this. She had never had any particular talents — except being good at math and science, after her first visit to Mathematics — and it was difficult to consider herself as one of the most powerful beings in this strange and wonderful world.

"Maybe we should have found some more Humans to help us," she told Al.

"There aren't any more, at least not here," Al countered. "The

Mathematician sent them all home when things started getting really bad. He didn't want to put them in danger."

"Oh, that's good. Instead, I'll just put *myself* in danger." She sighed and tried concentrating again, as she had with the coal. *Solidness*, she thought firmly. *All the atoms must be close together and not move around too much, like they do in a liquid. What else is it about atoms in a solid? ... Dense. Solids are denser than liquids. And colder.* She paused, reflecting that she'd had plenty of recent experience with low temperatures.

Fine. All she had to do was make herself more dense and colder. Solid. Right.

"Okay," she stated out loud, "I want this ... soda to stay solid." She drew out her bottle of frozen soda, took a deep breath, and walked to the beginning of the mercury path. She slowly held the bottle out into the region that was presumably Liquid. A ripple seemed to pass over it as she extended it about a foot and a half from her body — that must be where Liquid began — but as she concentrated on *dense* and *solid*, it did not change.

"I think I'm doing it, Al!" she exclaimed. Because the bottle was in Liquid, it ought to be liquid ... but it wasn't. Experimenting, Julie kept concentrating on the bottle itself, but relaxed about the soda inside. Gradually, as if confused, the soda became soft and sloshed toward the bottom of the bottle.

"I *am!*" she cried.

"Wonderful," Al remarked. "But you look like you're straining. Are you going to have to concentrate so hard all the time?"

"I hope not."

"Climb up on my back."

Julie did so, took a deep breath, and closed her eyes, trying to imagine an invisible area around her that was solid. *Dense atoms packed together, vibrating and rotating but unable to get free....* "Walk forward, Al."

Al hesitated for a microsecond, then did so. A tingling sensation washed over them. When Julie opened her eyes, they were standing on the mercury.

"I made the mercury solid!" she exclaimed.

"So it seems," agreed Al uneasily.

"I guess that's an extension of my 'ambiance.'"

"It's just science."

"Sort of," Julie acknowledged. She kept thinking the word *solid* but soon found that she didn't need to focus so hard on it. It seemed that her 'ambiance,' once created, stayed functional indefinitely. That was good news.

"Let's go, Al."

♀ ☾ ♂ ▽ ☿ ⊕

It didn't take long for them to reduce the mountains to thumbnail-sized cones in the distance. From time to time, they saw lion-triangle signposts made of mercury beside the path. The Chemy's star-marked paw prints remained, imbedded in the mercury, but eventually they changed into the rainbow prints she had seen in the forest of the Periodics Emeriti.

"That's pretty," Al remarked.

"I wonder where the others are?" Julie mused.

"Well, Bromine is somewhere here … possibly Aurum and Chromium are here, too, wandering around, looking for us. The Isotopes are waiting inside Gas. The Chemy's probably here somewhere, too."

Julie felt unprotected, but she trusted that the Chemy was making a good enough diversion that the wolframs were following him. She and Al would be in trouble if even a small pack found them.

A little while later, she asked, "What do you suppose these elements are?"

Al turned his head as he galloped onward. "The blue is probably water, reflecting the color of the sky. The white, hydrogen. Probably. I don't know. I'm not like the Periodics, who can tell at a glance."

Suddenly the path ahead was submerged beneath a flowing wash of reds, whites, and browns.

"What is this?" Julie demanded. She jumped down, and with Al close beside her, examined the liquids spilling over the path. They became solid beneath her hand. "Al, do you see the path resume anywhere ahead?"

"No," replied Al, craning his neck.

"The wolframs again," she growled. "This is terrible! First they block the path, then they hide it!"

"And unless we stick to the path, we won't be able to enter Gas," Al reminded her.

Julie sighed. "I guess it's on to the last path, then. Let's hope it's still intact." She peered forward. "Look, the prints go that way."

Al nodded, turning his head in the direction she pointed. She remounted him and, with some misgiving, he stepped off the path to one side. As his hooves touched the glowing red liquid rock, he met resistance. The lava had solidified.

"Do you feel the heat?" Julie inquired.

"No. Nothing. It feels like rock."

"I guess it is rock," Julie said, "when it's around us." She peered down and saw that the lava in a small area surrounding them had become light-colored igneous rock. "This Human stuff is cool."

Al nodded. "Cool enough to keep us alive," he said, with a nervous edge to his voice. He bunched his muscles and galloped across the multi-hued plain before them, shying away from the brighter glowing pools when he could. "I hope you realize the faith this is taking," he muttered once.

Julie responded with a hug around his neck. He seemed a little brighter after that.

Julie felt vertigo when she looked down, but out of fascination, she looked anyway. Right before Al's hooves made contact with them, pools of water became ice, lava became dark and light rock, and mercury hardened into an instant mirror. Once Al leaped over a particularly radiant pool and came down upon a patch of red and yellow lava. With a shock, it hardened instantly into black obsidian.

♀ ☾ ♂ ▽ ☿ ⊕

It was over an hour before they reached the next path. Throughout their travel, the rainbow prints stood out brightly against all shades of liquid. As they journeyed across the smooth mercury, Al seemed much happier.

"This is *supposed* to be liquid," he explained. "It's room temperature, naturally."

The first signpost they encountered depicted a bull whose horns supported a triangle pointing upward, without any horizontal bars.

"I would guess that the bull means Earth, but I know Earth is supposed to be the eagle," Julie grumbled. "I have no idea what path this is."

"Me neither."

Faint ripples began running down the path from behind them, terminating at the invisible border of Julie's influence.

After a moment, a glinting gold figure appeared. Al came to a halt, and the figure soon caught up with them.

"I'm so glad I found you!" Aurum exclaimed, panting from his swift run. He was glowing brighter than Julie had ever seen him, a brilliant yellow sheen on his darker yellow coat. "After I found the Air Path blocked, I came to the Fire Path, but Chromium is nowhere to be seen! Neither is Bromine. Where is the Chemy?"

"Leading a diversion," Julie replied. "Is Chromium supposed to be here?"

"Yes."

"I hope he hasn't been captured by wolframs," Julie fretted.

"More likely he's wandered to another path, to look for you. It's only by chance I saw you coming across the terrain and ran to intercept you."

"Come here," Julie bade him. "I want to touch you."

She was curious as to what Aurum would feel like in the liquid state, but discovered to her disappointment that the skin she touched felt like the solid skin she was used to.

Aurum's eyes grew wide as she touched him. "You're controlling my state!" he exclaimed. "You shouldn't be able to do that!"

"She's getting pretty good, huh?" Al commented.

Aurum shook his head as if trying to clear it. "Strange," he murmured, backing off a few steps. The patch of skin Julie had just touched vibrated momentarily, as if Aurum were shaking off a fly.

"Let's keep going," Julie suggested.

"What are these colorful circles?" Aurum asked.

"The Chemy's paw prints. He's colored them so I can follow him. I think he's half-keeping an eye on me."

$$♀ ☽ ♂ ▽ ☿ ⊕$$

They traveled in silence toward Gas. Warm breezes brushed past Julie's face, and she enjoyed the feeling after the chill of the past several days.

They passed another signpost and Julie had a thought. "Aurum," she called, "you said this was the Fire Path, right? With the bull?"

"Yep."

"Then what is the path in that direction?" She pointed toward the path they had found submerged, the third path they had tried.

"That's Air."

"Of course. That makes sense. I remember we entered on Earth, and the Chemy led me to Water."

"What was wrong with that one?" Aurum asked.

"Another rock slide blocked it off, and we couldn't go around because of these deep chasms on either side."

"Wolframs," Aurum said, shaking his mane in disgust.

"... Hey, Al," Julie called, after a few minutes' riding.

"Yes?" Al responded instantly.

"I wonder why I didn't make the air around us solid."

Al seemed shocked at the idea. "Well, I don't know, but I'm glad you didn't."

"Maybe because I concentrated on making liquid solid."

"Maybe."

"So what do we do when we get to Gas?"

"What do you mean?"

"Well, we've got to have air to breathe, but we've got to make the gas solid enough to walk on. At least I assume we do."

"Uh-oh." Al galloped onward for a while before remarking, "Well, we'll just have to see when we get there."

8
The Gas State

T_{HE SUN} was getting low ahead of them, slightly to their left, as they neared Gas. The dark cloud had resolved into a multi-hued melange of opaque and translucent gases, all shifting languidly from internal currents. Now, as the sun shone through it, every color imaginable was visible.

The rainbow prints continued on across the mercury until they were almost into Gas, when they shifted into brilliant white.

"That's new," Julie remarked. "He must be expecting us to get here when it's dark."

"It almost is," Al pointed out. "That Chemy is pretty clever."

"He is indeed," Aurum agreed. "Probably more clever than we believe."

They rode on for a while, with the bright white prints marking the way.

"Should we continue through the night?" Aurum asked.

"I don't think so," Julie asserted. "It's probably dangerous. But where can we sleep?"

"Well...." Aurum put some thought into it. "Tell you what: Find some liquid gold. With luck, and with your help, I'll be able to make it solid, and maybe I can fashion it with a hole to make a little cave."

"Okay," assented Julie, "but where will we find liquid gold?"

Aurum seemed to concentrate for a moment, then pointed off to the right of the path. "There's a very small patch over there, but nothing big enough or close enough to help us."

"That's bad."

"I guess we'd better keep following the prints," Al stated.

"Yeah."

They continued on in darkness, keeping to the single line of white spots. Soon they heard a faint roaring sound far ahead. As they continued, the roaring sound became louder. It sounded natural, but not made by any living being.

"It sounds like ... a waterfall," Julie hypothesized.

"Yes! That's it!" Aurum agreed. "I was just thinking that. But I don't remember...."

Then the prints ended and there was nothing but darkness beyond.

Fearful, they stepped up to the last print and saw the source of the sound. It was indeed a waterfall, flowing straight down off the side of Liquid. Far, far below, they heard it striking something solid.

"This must be the end of Liquid and the beginning of Gas," Julie said.

"Oh, yes," Aurum recalled, "I remember now. Yes, it is."

"Where does it go?"

"Go? Why, I don't know. Down to the bottom, I suppose."

"Is there a bottom?"

"There must be." Aurum gazed down over the edge. "There is rock beneath all that gas, just as there is rock beneath all this liquid. The States don't go on forever, you know."

Al peered over, but Julie was still on his back and so was unable to look anywhere but into the gray, shifting mass of Gas.

"I hate to tell you this, Julie," Al said, "but those white prints go down the side here."

"What?" Julie jumped down and peered over the edge. "How?" Very clearly, the white spots continued down the side of the waterfall, looking like stepping-stones in a stream as the water flowed around and under them. Stepping-stones....

"Al, I'm going to try walking on them."

"What!" Al grabbed the back of her shirt with his mouth, but she brushed him off.

"Don't worry; I think that's why they're here," she said. "Maybe we were supposed to be walking on them all the time. I'm going to see if they're solid."

"Then I'm going to hold on to you as you step over the edge." Al grabbed her shirt again.

Taking a deep breath, Julie gathered up all her courage and touched her foot on the nearest spot. It didn't move, and it seemed solid. She shifted her weight over the edge, trusting Al, and placed her other foot on the next spot. She was now standing horizontally, but gravity seemed to be pulling her into the waterfall, not toward the rock where the waterfall ended.

"Al," she murmured, "let go."

Reluctantly, Al obeyed. Julie remained suspended sideways, although it didn't *feel* sideways.

"Try it, Al," she urged.

Al made a strangled sound behind her but tried it. Julie took a few steps forward, giving him spots to stand on. When she looked back, he was trembling, standing upright on the waterfall. It looked exactly as if he was standing on flat stones in a rushing stream, except for the stars behind him.

Aurum followed them as they tiptoed down the waterfall in the darkness, following the line of prints. Despite Al's sweating and nervous comments, Julie found it quite natural. *It's just like walking down a stream,* she mused. *It's too dark to see the bottom, after all.*

Julie knew it was nearly midnight before they reached the bottom. The passage had taken longer than she expected, and she shuddered to think what height she had descended, step by step, that night. But the black vertical wall extending before her — the floor of Gas — caused more anxiety than relief in her, because she knew they were one stage closer to Tungsten and whatever he had planned.

The Gas State

♀ ☽ ♂ ▽ ☿ ⊕

They argued briefly over where to sleep. No one wanted to sleep in the open, but they did not know of any shelter nearby. None of them had ever been here before, and they were all too overtaxed to think clearly. Finally Julie just started across the floor, through the thick fog of multiple gases, and Al and Aurum hurried after her.

They wandered through the fog for what seemed like hours. Julie, lacking any sense of direction, began to get agitated, then angry, then scared. They were lost, and she was feeling more dizzy with every passing step.

Something swirled in the fog ahead, a dark shape among the light-colored clouds. A deep voice sprang into her mind.

"HUMAN JULIE?"

Julie, feeling a wave of vertigo, staggered toward the form. Al rushed to her and supported her as she faced the figure. She couldn't make out any shape. In the darkness, it looked like a charcoal-colored patch of smoke in the mist.

"Who are you?" she asked.

The figure shifted and began to drift toward them. "YOU HAVE SEEN ME BEFORE. I CAME TO THE PERIODIC COUNCIL TO TELL OF WOLFRAM'S WHEREABOUTS."

"Oh, the mysterious one." Julie rubbed the back of her hand against her forehead. Her thoughts were beginning to trip over each other and run together into a confusing mess.

"You will need shelter until morning. Please follow me."

Julie began to stumble after the receding smoke figure, but Al thrust himself up under her, and Aurum nosed her lengthwise across him. Julie sensed the ground bouncing around about three feet from her nose, but she wasn't sure how it was doing that. Then, after a few moments, even that faded to blackness.

Julie awoke in a half-lit room. She blinked, feeling groggy, and tried to find the source of the light. It was a directionless light seeming to filter from all around, a soft, white light.

"Thank goodness!" she heard Al exclaim, and she turned her head to see him lying curled up against a dark gray wall.

"Where am I?"

"You're inside the Pedestal," Al replied. "It juts up from the floor, at the center of Gas, to Plasma. Plasma is in the middle of Gas."

Julie realized that she was sweating. "It sure is hot!"

"Yes."

She turned her head toward the sound of Aurum's voice and saw him across the room from Al, to her left. The room was circular — more like an oval, longer than it was wide.

The light darkened and Julie's gaze was drawn to the rectangular doorway, which framed a dark horse. A panel of glass slid shut behind him.

"I AM HEARTENED TO SEE YOU CONSCIOUS," he stated formally. "THERE WAS A QUESTION OF YOUR RETURN."

"What?"

Aurum gave a sort of harrumphing sound. "It seems there was not enough oxygen gas out there to support Human life," he explained. He sounded apologetic.

The dark horse approached her, taking on a more definite equine shape.

"What is your name?" Julie asked, noting that he bore no letters on his haunches to proclaim his elemental symbol.

"I HAVE NO NAME," the horse replied. "I ... ONCE WAS CALLED EKA-SILICON."

"What?" Julie still felt muddled, but as she stretched, she felt a little better.

"EKA-SILICON. I ... HAVE BEEN CHANGED."

"How?"

The horse looked upward, his glowing red eyes narrowing with a mixture of anger, fear, and internal pain. "WOLFRAM. HE'S ... I WAS AN EXPERIMENT...." The horse's gaze returned to them. "HE CREATED ME BY MERGING WHAT I ONCE WAS WITH WHAT WAS ONCE EKA-CESIUM."

"Eka-cesium? What happened to him?"

"HE ... IS NO LONGER CONSCIOUS. WHEN HE WAS MERGED WITH ME, I THINK HE JUST GAVE UP ENTIRELY. HE NEVER WAS VERY STRONG."

"Merged? I don't understand."

"WOLFRAM CAPTURED ME AND PUT ME INTO THE PLASMA

STATE, WHERE I WAS TRAPPED BY TREMENDOUS FORCES. MY HAIR WAS ALL TORN OFF, AND I WAS NEARLY RIPPED APART. THEN HE FOUND EKA-CESIUM ... I CAN'T IMAGINE WHERE ... I HAVEN'T SEEN HIM MYSELF FOR CENTURIES ... AND THREW HIM IN THERE WITH ME. WE ... FUSED."

"Fusion!" Aurum was on his feet in that instant.

"But why?"

The Periodic shook his head. "I DON'T KNOW WHY. I'M NOT SURE...." His voice fell in volume. "... I THINK HE PLANS TO MERGE HIMSELF WITH SOMETHING, BUT I DON'T KNOW WHAT. ONE THING I DO KNOW: HE CAPTURED HYDROGEN BECAUSE SHE UNDERSTANDS FUSION. HE WANTS INFORMATION. HE WANTED ME TO TELL HIM ABOUT IT, BUT I REFUSED AND ESCAPED, AND I RAN TO TELL THE COUNCIL WHERE HE WAS. I — I'M A LOT MORE POWERFUL THAN I WAS BEFORE. I'M ... STRONGER. AND ... I HAVE ALL THIS SCIENTIFIC INFORMATION IN MY HEAD THAT NEVER WAS THERE BEFORE.... LIKE THE SHAPE OF ORBITALS WITHIN AN ATOM...."

"But who are you? Are you a Periodic?"

"I GUESS I AM."

"I know who you are — or were, rather," Aurum stated.

Al's ears perked forward. "Who?"

Aurum turned to him. "Eka-silicon was an element proposed by Dmitri Mendeleev, when he set about organizing the elements into the first Periodic Table. There was too great a mass difference between silicon and tin, so he knew there had to be an element between them, in that column. But no such element had yet been discovered, so he left a space and named that unknown element Eka-silicon. However, when that element was discovered, it was named Germanium. That happened right after I left."

"So you're a Periodic Emeritus, like Aurum!" Julie exclaimed.

"No." The huge Periodic suddenly looked forlorn. "I DID NOT EXIST IN A CHEMICAL STATE IN A HUMAN LABORATORY. I WAS NEVER SINGLED OUT AND NAMED AND RECOGNIZED, EXCEPT IN THEORY. I WAS NEVER GIVEN ISOTOPES OR EVEN AN ATOMIC NUMBER. JUST A MASS NUMBER, BECAUSE THAT'S WHAT MENDELEEV USED TO ORGANIZE HIS CHART."

"I disagree," Aurum said. "I think you're a Periodic, all the same."

"WELL, I AM NOW." The former Eka-silicon straightened proudly. "I STILL DON'T HAVE A RECOGNIZED NAME, THOUGH." Suddenly he turned to Julie. "YOU ARE HUMAN. GIVE ME A NAME."

"What?" Julie blinked. "I can't do that. Only the person who discovers you can."

"YOU JUST DISCOVERED ME, IN THE MIST."

"That doesn't count!"

"WHAT ABOUT A TEMPORARY NAME, THEN?"

"Well, Wolfram created you," Al suggested, "so maybe your name should sound like Wolfram. Wolfium?"

Julie looked at the dark Periodic. The huge horse seemed extremely anxious, and Julie realized that not being recognized had been his greatest shame ever since he'd been named by Mendeleev.

"What about Mendeleev-ium?" she said. "Or Wolfmendium? Mendelium? Wolendium? Wendium? Wendel — Wendeleevium?"

"WENDEL...." repeated the Periodic. "WENDELIUM."

"Wendelium?" echoed Julie.

"YES," decided the horse.

"Well, that's a fine name!" exclaimed Julie. "It seems you helped to name yourself. Wendelium. What would that atomic symbol be? Wl? Wn? Wd? Yes, Wd."

"YES." The horse paused. "HUMAN JULIE?"

"Yes?"

"COULD YOU.... WOULD YOU BE WILLING TO PLACE YOUR HAND ON MY SHOULDER AND SAY MY NEW NAME? SORT OF LIKE AN OFFICIAL NAMING CEREMONY?"

"What? Okay." Julie laid her hand flat on his warm side, just above his right foreleg, and said, "I hereby officially, temporarily name you Wendelium, atomic symbol Wd." She felt a tingle go through her, and when she lifted her hand away, a bright "Wd" was emblazoned on the Periodic's side in gold lettering.

The great Periodic threw back his head and reared upward, flashing his forehooves. "I FEEL POWERFUL!" he shouted. "WOLFRAM, JUST WAIT UNTIL I GET TO YOU!" He placed all four hooves on the ground again. "LET'S GO TEACH THAT WOLFRAM NOT TO MESS WITH OTHER PERIODICS!"

Aurum looked amused while Al looked awestruck. Julie had the feeling that she had just created a mighty ally.

The Gas State

♀ ☾ ♂ ▽ ☿ ⊕

They had a hurried breakfast, then Julie emerged into the State of Gas.

"AVOID THE YELLOW-GREEN PATCHES," Wendelium advised her, "FOR THEY ARE CHLORINE AND FLUORINE. HIGHLY TOXIC. OH, AND — STOP! YOU'RE ABOUT TO WALK INTO.... NEVER MIND. I SHALL LEAD YOU." The great Periodic gently pushed Julie to one side.

"I didn't see anything," Julie said.

"NO. IT WAS HARD TO SEE. NITROUS OXIDE."

Aurum chuckled and Julie looked toward him. "Laughing gas," he explained, still cheerful.

"I think you walked into a patch," Julie accused him.

"What? No. Periodics can't be affected unless they allow it."

"EXCEPT IN PLASMA," Wendelium muttered.

They walked halfway around the outside of the room, and Julie peered up until the fog shrouded its gray length far above. It seemed to go on forever.

She turned back to the base and sighted a broad stairway that wound its way counterclockwise up the inside of the pedestal.

"I was wondering how we were going to get up," she commented as they mounted the bottom step. "Hey! There's a paw print here!"

"Good," remarked Al. "That means we're still following him."

"HIM WHO?" inquired Wendelium.

"Al the Chemy-lion. He's come to fight Wolfram, like we have. Well, actually, to find out where Hydrogen is. Fighting Wolfram became part of the plan after Wolfram started making it so hard to follow him."

"I DON'T RECALL SEEING THIS CHEMY-LION," mused the newly named Periodic.

"I would be surprised if you had," Aurum observed.

"He blends in very well with his environment," Julie offered, as Aurum gave no further explanation.

"AH. NOW I SEE."

They followed the steps for what seemed like hours. Every once in a while Julie would pause, short of breath, and Wendelium would seek out an oxygen patch for her. She wasn't sure how he brought it to the stairs, but she didn't complain.

Once, as they were walking, a horrible smell pervaded the air around them.

"Oh!" Julie exclaimed in disgust. "What is that awful stench?"

Wendelium took a whiff, then seemed to choke, his eyes bulging. "THAT'S HYDROGEN SULFIDE!"

"It smells like a thousand rotten eggs," gagged Al as they hurried upward out of the putrid area.

The Gas State

♀ ☾ ♂ ▽ ☿ ⊕

It took a long time to near the top of the pedestal. They slowed as it came into view, far above, and approached with more stealth, but there really was nowhere to hide. Julie looked upward apprehensively but didn't see anyone looking back at them over the edge. Just then they sighted the Chemy himself, sitting calmly on the stairs above them.

"Greetings," he addressed them. "The end of our quest nears."

"So this is the Chemy you were talking about," said Wendelium, gazing at the beast who merged perfectly with the gray of the stairs. "I see what you mean."

The Chemy eyed the newcomer. "You have been created," he stated, "from base metals."

Wendelium nodded.

The Chemy seemed to consider that fact for several moments while the others waited patiently. "This has been done by Wolfram?"

Wendelium nodded again.

"Wolfram is experimenting with the art of transforming," the Chemy growled. "That is not acceptable. The only alchemy which shall be practiced around here shall be practiced by one." He stood and began pacing upwards, around and around the column of stone, still leaving behind his white prints. They followed silently.

♀ ☾ ♂ ▽ ☿ ⊕

It didn't take them much longer to reach the top at the angry pace the Chemy was setting. They soon climbed onto the broad, flat expanse.

As Julie came over the edge, she was blinded by a brilliant ball of red, marbled with orange and yellow, floating some ten feet above the surface of the column. It was about twenty feet in diameter and pulsed slightly.

Julie shielded her eyes and squinted, looking around. Beneath the ball of fire was what appeared to be a large, rectangular stone, reaching up almost into the sphere. She strained, trying to see, and found herself thinking about her eyes. *When too much light is around, the muscles of the iris contract, letting less light into the eye....* Suddenly the sphere of light seemed to grow dimmer and she could see without as much trouble — although she didn't much like what she saw.

Hydrogen was nearby, with a strap around one hind leg that was staked into the top of the pedestal. The shape beneath the ball was indeed a large stone, and on the other side was —

"WOLFRAM!" Wendelium let out an equine scream and charged toward the massive, metallic gray Periodic they had all been hunting for such a long time.

Wolfram's head jerked up, the whites of his pupils showing. He let out a whinny and six wolframs charged out from behind the stone. They threw themselves at Wendelium, harrying him until his charge came to a dragging end as he kicked out at the vicious animals.

"Stop this!" the Chemy ordered, and as one the wolframs and Wendelium froze.

"Now, if only I could get results like that," reflected Aurum.

"You do," Julie pointed out.

"Wolfram," Aurum called, "why have you kidnapped our friend Hydrogen?"

Wolfram's face broke into a wide smile, his eyes unfocused and blank. "Hydrogen understands the Process."

"What Process?"

"The Unification Process!"

"He means fusion!" called Hydrogen, sounding tired.

"Fusion," Aurum stated, walking carefully forward. "Is it true, Wolfram, that you have captured your brother Tungsten?"

"Yes."

"Why? You have caused his Implied Permission to stop functioning by cutting him off from the Human world. All of the Tungsten there has lost its usefulness, its properties. Why did you do it?"

Wolfram cackled and took several steps toward them, his eyes scanning the group. "I shall learn the Process!" he shouted. "And I shall be the Perfect Metal!"

The Chemy-lion growled and Wolfram turned on him. "You doubt me?" he demanded. "I *shall!*"

"Just how do you intend to do this?" Aurum inquired. "I mean, I don't doubt that you can, but it seems a difficult thing to achieve...."

"Oh, it is, it is!" exclaimed Wolfram, swinging toward the golden Periodic. "But I can. My brother, Tungsten, my replacement, Tungsten, awaits me in the Plasma State. I shall join with Tungsten! I shall *be* Tungsten! I shall be the greatest Periodic ever made!"

"Certainly the largest," Al breathed. "Can you imagine.... Their masses added together...."

"Wolfram intends to transmute himself into the Perfect Metal, using the Fire," rumbled the Chemy-lion. "This shall not be allowed."

Wolfram whirled on him. "Yes! Perfection awaits! And how do you intend to stop me?"

The Chemy paced toward him until he was standing between the mentally unstable Periodic and the Plasma State. "Wolfram may not enter."

"I may not enter? I *shall* enter!" Wolfram's eyes had gone unfocused again, and he stomped at the ground. "I have the highest melting point of any metal! I can resist the fires of Plasma without effort! I AM the Quintessence!"

"Oh, boy," breathed Al.

The Chemy snarled, but Julie suddenly realized it was a laugh. The beast sat calmly between Wolfram and the Plasma State, the tip of his tail twitching. "Human Julie," he stated after a moment, "you must use the Philosopher's Stone to enter the Fire and retrieve Tungsten."

"She can't!" Wolfram screamed. "She will be destroyed! Do not tamper with Powers you do not understand!"

"Exactly." The Chemy-lion's tail gave an extra large twitch.

"Julie, don't do it!" Al pleaded as she moved toward the large rock — presumably the "Philosopher's Stone" the Chemy had mentioned.

"I have to, Al," Julie said. "We have to get Tungsten out of there anyway. Then, even if Wolfram goes into the Plasma State, he won't be able to join with anyone to form a super-Periodic." She walked toward the dazzling sphere, climbed the first couple of stairs leading up the length of the Philosopher's Stone, then stopped. If she ever needed her Human powers, it was now. She had to focus on ... not becoming plasma. On keeping her form. That was a start.

"Wait, Human," came the Chemy's voice from behind her. "The Human cannot do this alone. The Human understands the science of the act, but not the deeper nature.... One can control the Fire much better than the Human, and also the change of state. One understands it. Take hold of one's tail and concentrate!"

Julie half-closed her eyes, forcing herself to think about not being shriveled up and disintegrated into a trillion little less-than-atoms by the destructive force of Plasma. The Chemy pushed past her and she grabbed his tail, being towed forward, hearing her heart pound furiously in her ears.

9
Plasma

IT WAS ALL bright red. Yellow streaks flashed past her and currents swirled around, but Julie was oblivious to most of it. She had a sensation of tremendous, enveloping heat but was not affected by it. She found herself floating and looked up quickly to make sure she still grasped the Chemy's tail. The beast glanced back at her, then drifted toward a solitary figure hunched in the bright light. It was light gray, a hairless horse looking miserable and half-dead.

"Are you Tungsten?" Julie asked.

The horse fixed her with a weary look, his black eyes reflecting the red illumination. Slowly, he nodded.

Julie hooked one arm around his neck, still clutching the tuft of tail hair in her fist. "Pull us out, Chemy."

The Chemy plunged through the nearest wall, and Julie felt herself break through as well, with some resistance. However, when she tried to pull Tungsten through, she met a plastic sort of surface tension, and the wall of Plasma flexed with her effort. The Chemy pulled her to one side and she felt a solid substance beneath her feet.

The Philosopher's Stone, she thought as she thrust both arms into Plasma, hooked them around Tungsten's neck, and hauled with all her strength. Plasma stretched out toward her like a pulled balloon.

"Change of state is not always easy," the Chemy purred in her ear. "One can keep Tungsten from being disintegrated as the Human pulls him from the Fire. However, one cannot change his state, for one does not know the atomic process."

Julie paused a moment for breath. "When a liquid becomes a solid, it cools down.... It loses heat energy, really. Same thing when a gas becomes a liquid. So ... does that mean all he has to do is cool down and lose energy?" *No*, she realized. *Energy.... His electrons have been spread around the outside of Plasma. He has to reclaim those as well!*

Keeping in mind what had to happen chemically in order to bring Tungsten back to the Gas State, she gathered her strength and pulled as hard as she could. With a pop and a brilliant flash of light, Tungsten's head emerged from inside Plasma and he slid forward, bringing a slight coating of Plasma's outer skin with him.

Once he was resting on the Philosopher's Stone, Julie realized that the Plasma skin had transformed into Tungsten's white-speckled, light gray hair.

Julie looked at the Chemy triumphantly.

"This is not yet terminated," the Chemy breathed. "Wolfram must be cured of his insanity or be destroyed."

Julie half-turned and surveyed the scene below her. Wolfram had arrayed his wolframs around her companions, effectively immobilizing them and cutting them off from her. She released Tungsten, who remained where he lay, unmoving, although he was still breathing.

"And so you see!" cackled Wolfram. "You may have Tungsten now, but I have your friends! What now, O great beast of the past?"

The Chemy growled savagely in response. "Human," he murmured then, "one shall give you a signal, a visible signal, and when that signal is seen, Wolfram must be forced into Plasma. If Wolfram wishes to taste Quintessence, he shall." With that, the Chemy bounded down from the Stone before Julie could ask him what the signal would look like. She hoped she would be able to tell.

She remained where she was, next to several white paw prints where the Chemy had stood. The paw prints continued on the ground toward Wolfram, the last one about three inches behind the Chemy's rearmost hind leg as he crouched before the dangerous Periodic.

"Tungsten," she whispered. There came no response, but she thought she saw one eyelid flutter. "Tungsten, we have to get off the Stone. I may have to use it to push Wolfram into Plasma . . . however I'm going to do that."

Tungsten wearily lifted his head, his black eyes focusing for a moment on hers. In that moment he seemed frail and vulnerable, incapable of having caused any of this mischief. Julie felt pity well up in her throat. Tungsten was, she noted, a hair smaller than Aurum, about medium-sized for a Periodic.

"How did you get involved in this?" she asked him.

He closed his eyes for a moment, then reopened them. "He – Wolfram – spoke of becoming very powerful, of being able to do just about anything. He mentioned creating a new Periodic. I didn't know he meant that he and I together would be that Periodic. I should have known he was crazy."

"Then you came here willingly to become more powerful than your comrades?"

Tungsten nodded. "I fear it is so. Now, however, I have, as they say, thoroughly learned my lesson. I no longer desire any such thing. I just want to go home."

"Let's get off this Stone," Julie said.

They climbed down, and Julie turned to see the Chemy darting in and out of Wolfram's reach as the latter stomped about.

"What in the Human world is he doing?" inquired Tungsten.

"I believe he's trying to lead Wolfram toward Plasma."

Tungsten looked alarmed. "No one should be exposed to that! What is that supposed to do?"

"I'm not sure," Julie admitted. "But I know it will trap him there. Maybe we'll just wait until reinforcements come."

Tungsten shook his head, sinking to the ground behind the Stone.

Julie watched Wolfram chase the Chemy around and around in a tight circle until the large former Periodic fell to his knees. She climbed back up on the Philosopher's Stone. It was the only easy way to get into Plasma, and she knew she had to be ready to do ... something ... to make Wolfram enter Plasma.

Wolfram staggered to his feet, full of rage.

If he were a dragon, Julie reflected, *he'd be spitting fire by now.*

The Chemy made a strafing run on the disoriented former Periodic, swerving aside at the last moment and racing past. Wolfram turned as if to follow, staggered a few steps, then came to a standstill. The Chemy, still leaving white prints, turned and made another charge toward Wolfram and ... disappeared.

Julie blinked, and a flash of color on the ground caught her eye. Brilliant red paw prints began where the white ones ended and continued past Wolfram up to the base of the Philosopher's Stone. She knew with absolute certainty that this was her cue.

"Up here, you stupid, ugly, bygone Periodic!" she shouted, waving her arms. "You crazy future glue package! You've been hit in the head with a few too many electrons," she added, recalling Aurum's comment.

Wolfram, enraged, gritted his teeth and charged at her. As he reached the base of the Stone, the Chemy must have thrown him upwards, for, wide-eyed, he abruptly took flight, missed Julie's head by inches, and smacked into Plasma with a blinding burst of light.

Then everything was silent.

The Chemy reappeared and leaped up on the Stone beside Julie. Now he left no tracks.

"Excellent work, Human," he purred. "One thinks Wolfram will pose no more problems."

"Oh?" Julie turned toward him.

He nodded. "Wolfram may be freed, in fact."

"How is that so?"

"He has been healed."

Julie looked up at Plasma. "How?" she repeated.

The Chemy disappeared into Plasma without replying and emerged a few moments later. "The Human must reach in her arms and help Wolfram out."

Dubious, Julie reached in, felt warm flesh, and grasped what felt like a foreleg. She pulled, trying to think about changing Wolfram back into a gas, and the ancient Periodic emerged a moment later with another explosion of light. These Human powers — although she still wasn't sure what they were — got easier the more one used them.

She stepped back as Wolfram, panting and trembling, pulled himself together and stood uncertainly.

"How are you?" she inquired.

Wolfram's dark eyes turned toward her. "I feel ... better," he admitted.

"And what about becoming the Perfect Metal?"

A blank expression came over Wolfram's face. "A ridiculous idea, wasn't it?"

Wolfram looked over at Tungsten and the two exchanged a long glance.

"No more of this, then?" breathed the exhausted Tungsten.

Wolfram nodded, and Tungsten seemed satisfied. He closed his eyes again to rest.

The wolframs gathered off to one side of the platform, looking confused and yipping amongst themselves.

Julie looked down at the Chemy, puzzled. "How did Plasma fix him?"

The Chemy shrugged. "I know only of Balance, if not between Fire, Earth, Air, and Water, then of other elements; and of Transformation from state to state."

Julie rolled her eyes. "You know, I think that's one of the most ambiguous answers you've given me yet!"

The Chemy shrugged again.

Hydrogen limped up to them, favoring the hind leg which had been tethered. "I have a theory," she called.

"Yes, I do, too." Aurum called in jest. "Wolfram was hit in the head by too many electrons! Julie, I can't believe you said that to him!" His eyes twinkled.

Julie ran down the steps of the Stone and threw her arms around her diminutive friend. "Are you all right, Hydrogen?"

"Yes. Here is my theory. I think Aurum's right."

"What?" exclaimed Aurum.

"You're right," replied Hydrogen. "Wolfram left his office after the X-ray machine was invented, did he not?"

Aurum thought for a moment. "I believe so."

"Well, I think that's exactly what happened to him. I mean, what happens to a Periodic's element happens to the Periodic, and vice-versa, right?"

"Right," Aurum agreed.

"Well, I think that the electrons aimed at the tungsten target in an X-ray machine may cause a disturbance in the tungsten atoms' quarks and other subatomic particles, particularly the leptons that comprise the tungsten atoms' electrons."

"Quarks? Leptons?" Julie looked from Hydrogen to Aurum.

"They are particles smaller than electrons that make up electrons, protons, neutrons, and the other subatomic particles you usually hear about," Hydrogen explained. "They are theoretical, of course. When the tungsten atoms' leptons were thrown out of synch, I think that may have affected Wolfram's mind."

Tungsten wearily got to his feet. "I think the electron bombardment also affects the rotation of my electrons," he stated. "That may have affected Wolfram as well. It doesn't affect me, because I've always had to deal with it, ever since taking the office. I guess I just developed an immediate immunity. But he didn't."

"If that's what caused his insanity, I doubt you're fully immune," Hydrogen declared. "I'd keep a watch on your sanity, if I were you. In fact, I think *I'll* keep a watch on your sanity."

There was a clatter of hooves, and Chromium and Bromine came up over the top of the platform. Seeing the tired Tungsten and the calm Wolfram, now surrounded by his pack of wolframs, they winced.

"We missed all the excitement, didn't we?" Chromium asked.

"Yes, I'm afraid so," Hydrogen replied. "But we've got a new theory on how electron bombardment may affect quarks." She outlined their ideas, and Chromium and Bromine nodded thoughtfully.

"It's possible," Chromium commented.

"I think it's probably the cause," Bromine asserted. "It just *seems* right. We'll have to conduct tests to see if electron bombardment does that.... You know, it may also affect the nucleus. We definitely should run some tests."

$$\female \quad \leftmoon \quad \mars \quad \triangledown \quad \mercury \quad \oplus$$

On the way down the stairs, the group met Deuterium, Protium, and Tritium coming up.

"There you are!" Deuterium admonished. "We've been looking all over for you. You mean you went on and rescued Hydrogen without us?" He pushed past to Hydrogen, along with his brothers, and nuzzled her.

"Yes, and we cured Wolfram, too," Julie said.

Protium turned to her in surprise. "How did you do that?"

"We threw him into Plasma."

"And what did that accomplish?"

Julie scratched her head. "I'm not sure."

Hydrogen had a ready reply. "When Wolfram entered Plasma, all his electrons were torn off. This enabled the leptons which comprise those electrons to right themselves. Also, according to Tungsten's theory, when the electrons returned to Wolfram's body as he exited Plasma, their rotations were corrected."

The Isotopes absorbed this, eyeing Tungsten with mistrust. "And what about him?"

"Well, we don't know if he was crazy or not," Julie said, "but he was in Plasma, too, so he was cured as well. But we got him out before we threw Wolfram in."

"Why?" Tritium asked as they resumed their trek down the stairs.

"They would have fused," Aurum told him. "It wouldn't have been a pretty sight."

Suddenly Julie stopped on the path. "Guys, have you seen Wendelium?"

"Who?" asked Protium.

"Wendelium. Did anyone see where he went?"

Everyone shook their heads.

"I hope he's all right," Julie fretted.

"Oh, I'm sure he's not hurt," Hydrogen said.

"He'll rejoin us when he's ready," Aurum assured her. "Or when the world's ready for him."

10
The Aftermath

ABOUT HALFWAY down the pedestal, the Isotopes pointed out a strip of nitrogen that reached over into the Liquid State, an extension of the path. Julie hardened it into a solid and they walked across it. Once in Liquid, they followed the mercury path without incident, avoiding the areas that had been blockaded by the wolframs' efforts. Every time they came to a new scene of destruction, Wolfram looked sheepish.

"I don't suppose you could suggest to the Council that my only punishment be fixing these areas?" he sighed.

"Punishment?" Julie asked.

"Yes. I expect to be punished in some way for my misconduct. I'm not looking forward to it, but I expect it."

"I think that your punishment may be under the Mathematician's jurisdiction," Al said, "seeing that most of the damage was done within Mathematics."

Wolfram nodded.

$$♀ ☾ ♂ ▽ ☿ ⊕$$

They decided to head for the Elemental Forest anyway, since it was closer than the Mathematician's castle. Halfway across the plains that separated the two, they met a host of Periodics and Isotopes making their way through the tall grasses. Julie caught her breath at the sight of nearly one thousand horses bearing various forms of weapons and angry expressions.

"Wolfram has been cured of his insanity," Hydrogen announced, as the first ones to reach them began to speak of "having Wolfram's head."

"That's fine," argued Sodium, "but we don't really care. He still has to answer for what he's done." Julie recognized Sodium from her earlier adventure, his bright "Na," and his resemblance to Natrium.

"In modern court cases," Julie pointed out, "in the Human world, I mean, sometimes criminals can escape severe punishment by pleading insanity. That means they weren't responsible for their actions because they didn't know what they were doing."

"That sounds good," Wolfram stated.

"What about Tungsten?" demanded Fluorine, standing beside Bromine. "What about his part in all this?"

"I admit, I willingly went along with Wolfram at first, but he forced me when I tried to back out," Tungsten replied.

"An accomplice," Sodium accused him.

"You're just as guilty!" someone else cried.

"Remove them from their offices!" shouted another. Abruptly the chant was taken up: "Remove them! Remove them!"

"If we remove them from their respective offices," Aurum called, as a hush descended, "we must have someone else to replace them. Do we?"

A murmur rippled through the crowd.

"No," muttered a few voices, after a moment.

Aurum nodded. "Then we really can't —"

"Look!" shouted someone on the far edge of the crowd. "From the east! Imaginary Numbers!"

"Let me see!" cried Julie. "Al. . . ."

Al, anticipating her need, slipped to his knees so she could sit on him. He stood and, holding onto his mane for support, Julie straightened and looked out over the equine crowd. Silhouetted against the darkening sky was a large, pale group of amorphous beings. They were less than a mile away on the rolling flatlands and approaching fast.

"What would they want in Science?" asked Chromium. "They belong in Mathematics!"

"Don't be so literal," Hydrogen chided him. "You know our territories overlap! They're certainly allowed here if they wish."

"The question is," Argentum murmured, "what *do* they want?"

Even with the Imaginary Numbers' speed, it was almost dark

by the time they arrived. Squinting through the semi-dusk, Julie watched the indistinct beings as they made their way through the herd of Periodics and Isotopes. Some seemed vaguely humanoid, others equine in form. Still others took different shapes that Julie did not recognize. They all seemed to be seeking her.

"Human Julie!" called a familiar voice.

A single distinct figure emerged from the group, mounted on a tremendous Imaginary Horse that did nothing to bolster his own diminutive size.

"The Mathematician," Julie breathed. "Hello!" She leaped from Al's back — he lowered himself just in time, so she only jumped about a foot — and raced over to the short King of Math. She threw her arms about his neck in greeting, and he chuckled.

"Why does it seem that, if there's any trouble in Mathematics, you, Human Julie, are found at the center of it?" His neatly trimmed white beard had grown since she had last seen him, and it now concealed the monogrammed "м" on his rich blue robes.

"It must be luck," Julie returned. "How have you been?"

The Mathematician sighed, nodding at both Tungsten and Wolfram. "I've been better. But I expect I shall be again, shortly. We came to help the Periodics make war, but it seems there is no war to make. You have captured the two troublesome Periodics?" He began to climb down from his steed's back.

"Not just captured, but cured," Julie informed him. "We threw Wolfram into Plasma, which set his quarks right, or something like that. I'm still not sure what a quark is."

The Mathematician cast a doubtful glance in the captives' direction. "Cured?"

"Yes," Julie asserted.

"Well," sighed the Mathematician, clasping his hands behind his back and pacing toward the formerly rebellious Periodics, "that does not free you two of responsibility for your actions."

Tungsten and Wolfram nodded reluctantly.

"Please don't remove me from my office," Tungsten implored. "What shall I do then?"

"Don't take away my wolframs!" Wolfram importuned. "Please! I've raised them all from cubs. Lambs. Whatever. They won't know what to do without me!"

The Mathematician looked glum. "It is not entirely my position to mete punishment to you," he said. "Your Periodic and Periodic Emeriti Councils also have some stake in your fate." He waved a hand in front of his face. "It's so dark here. Does anyone have a source of light?"

"Light bulbs," Tungsten replied instantly. "If you happen to have a source of electricity, a filament of my element will glow in a vacuum —"

"No," answered Chromium. "You shouldn't ever use your powers again. You've abused them."

"I'll do it," offered Sodium. "Natrium, bring me those electrochemistree boughs we harvested.... Thanks." After a slight zap of bluish-white electricity, Sodium began emitting a soft yellow glow. Julie was reminded of the chemistry book lying on her bed, with its chapter headed "Forms of Light and the Elements." It had mentioned sodium's ability to emit light when its electrons received a jolt of energy, then released it. The light was the form that the released energy took. It was strange how things seemed to come back to her at odd times.

"Thank you," the Mathematician addressed Sodium. He turned back to the assembled Periodics and Isotopes. "I feel that removing their powers is a somewhat harsh castigation. If we were to be assured of their total cure, and that they would not abuse their powers again, I see no need to take those powers from them."

"How can we be sure?" someone demanded. "They can always sneak off, like they did before, and create mischief behind our backs!"

"We should assign someone to watch them," replied the Mathematician. "A parole officer, if you will."

"A what officer?" grumbled Bromine.

"I'll do it," Hydrogen offered.

The Mathematician looked thoughtfully at her. "Thank you, dear Hydrogen, but I fear we must choose someone who would be able to monitor them with absolute certainty. Someone who could follow them anywhere they might go and observe the results of their efforts."

"You speak as if you have someone in mind," Al commented.

"Yes, I do," the Mathematician replied, "in a general sort of way. I have in mind a Human. Any Human will do, but he or she would have to be one of my officially designated ambassadors." He sighed. "Unfortunately, all of my Human friends have retired back to their world to escape the danger of these two. And this situation calls for an immediate solution." He looked up at Julie. "I regret the necessity, but I must ask you ... Julie, would you be willing to take the job?"

"Me? An official ambassador? A parole officer?" Julie was aghast. "I wouldn't know what to do!"

"It's easy," the Mathematician replied. He motioned Tungsten and Wolfram forward, indicating that they should listen to his instructions as well.

"The two reprobates ... ah, probationed criminals ... will report to you twice a month for a year, then once a month for four years following that. You will listen to their reports of what they're doing, in this world and in yours, and confirm each one by direct observation. In addition, at your discretion, you will drop in on them from time to time, just to check them out. If you find anything amiss, even the slightest thing, you will inform me and the Periodic Council immediately, and steps will be taken from there."

Julie's head was whirling. "What about my homework?" was the first question that rose to the surface.

The Mathematician stepped back a pace to study her. "Remember, Julie, time can be manipulated. It's just another variable in the huge equation which this universe is. The duties of my other ambassadors do not impinge on their scientific and mathematical research; they simply manipulate the equation when they go home, to put themselves back in time to the moment after they left. It's not difficult. I'll show you how."

He scratched at his beard. "You *are* kind of young, though. Maybe I should choose another."

Just then the Chemy brushed Julie aside and seated himself between them, facing the Mathematician. "This Human is one of great ability," he purred.

Julie's short friend looked thunderstruck. "Albertus Leo Magnus! I haven't seen you in ... in centuries!" He cracked a huge smile and threw his arms around the furry beast, who smiled and butted his head against the Mathematician's blue robes.

"One is pleased to rejoin one's friend," the Chemy replied.

"How have you been?" the Mathematician asked, looking fondly at the Chemy-lion.

The Chemy shrugged. "Mainly ignored, in Human terms, but one observed this Human in need of assistance, and so emerged once more."

The Mathematician nodded. "Do you think she is qualified?"

The Chemy nodded sagely.

♀ ☾ ♂ ▽ ☿ ⊕

They journeyed back to the Elemental Forest, where Julie spent a couple of days associating with her friends. Early in the afternoon of the second day, she began to feel the pangs of homesickness. She sought out the Mathematician and said, "I think it's time for me to leave."

He whipped out paper and pencil and began outlining the necessary equations. Soon Julie had a headache and was getting grumpy. This was all too difficult for her.

"Now, stay with me, Julie," the Mathematician cajoled. "We're nearly halfway through. Listen, as a Human, you should be able to understand this without too much difficulty. Remember, your ability to comprehend math is heightened when you're here."

Julie took a deep breath and paid attention. To her surprise, she found that, with some practice, she could not only comprehend but manipulate the equations into the form she needed.

"No, no!" the Mathematician cried, interrupting her efforts. "You must subtract ten days from *both* sides of the equation. You're going to have to multiply by twenty-four, though, because earlier you defined that variable in terms of hours.... Good!"

After three hours, Julie had the equation she needed, fully reduced, added, divided, squared, and whatever else she had to do to get it right. She hugged her friends and planted a special kiss on Al's nose, promising to return within a few weeks. As she bade farewell to the Chemy, he behaved peculiarly. Pacing into the forest, he commented, "One shall resume one's life of obscurity. The Human probably shall not be able to locate one again. Farewell...." With that, he faded into the undergrowth.

Julie, puzzled, returned to the task at hand. Holding her equation in both hands, she said, "Equation, I invoke you!" as the Mathematician had instructed. There came a flash of light, darkness, and suddenly....

♀ ☽ ♂ ▽ ☿ ⊕

She was in her room. She was lying on her bed, and something hard was underneath her head.

She sat up, knocking her chemistry book to the floor, and looked around the room. Nothing had changed ... except that the lights were on, blazing brightly.

A thought occurred to her. If she had rescued Tungsten eight days into the future, *how was it that the tungsten in her world was working now?* How did that work?

She got out of bed, bringing her bookbag with her. She emptied it of pocket-knife, jacket, and empty bottle — the relics remaining after her adventure — then delved into her pockets out of habit. She felt some sort of scratchy, paper-like substance in her left pocket and drew it out.

It was the leaves she had picked up from the Chemistree glade on her first day in Science. She held one up to her reading light. The little "E," "A," "F", and "W" were plainly visible in the corners, but there was a faint mark in the center as well. It appeared to be a tiny round circle with an "x" through it.... no, it was a circled plus sign. The lines ran parallel and perpendicular to the stem of the leaf.

Suddenly Julie knew what the letters meant. *E for Earth,* she thought. *A for Air, F for Fire, W for Water ... and the last was for the Quintessence.* Smiling, she tucked the leaves into her chemistry book, flopped down on her bed, and resumed reading her homework — "Forms of Light and the Elements."

Epilogue

A SLIGHT DISTURBANCE in the air caused Julie to look up. It hadn't been a sound, exactly, but it was ... *something*. An image of a light bulb sprang into her head, followed by a picture of Tungsten.

She turned in her seat and nearly jumped on top of the desk. Tungsten was standing behind her!

"Tungsten, don't *ever* sneak up on me again!" she exclaimed.

"I'm sorry," the Periodic apologized, "but the Mathematician said this would be a good time for our first meeting. Wolfram will come next week at this time."

Julie composed herself as best she could, waiting for her heart to slow down. The Periodic seemed much too large for her room.

"Okay," she said, "what have you been doing lately?"

"Well, the Mathematician has ordered Wolfram to repair the damage he and his wolframs did in Mathematics and Science, and then to patrol the official pathways with his wolframs to keep them safe. I have been ordered to continue my duties in monitoring the Humans' advancements using my element. In addition, I've been instructed to help them develop a new use for my element, so you should be hearing about that very soon. If they get the hint."

"Have you seen anything of the Chemy?" Julie asked.

"No."

"What about Wendelium?"

"Who?"

"The super-Periodic you two made by uniting Eka-silicon with Eka-aluminum, or Eka-cesium, or something."

Tungsten looked baffled for a moment. "Wolfram and I did make a super-Periodic using Eka-silicon, but no other element was involved."

"What? Then how was Wendelium created?"

Tungsten shook his head. "When we put Eka-silicon into Plasma, he was instantly bombarded by high-level radiation. Hydrogen nuclei, mainly. That's why we needed Hydrogen. She could control the nuclei to prevent them from undergoing fusion with me. Wolfram wanted to merge with me, you remember, and he didn't want me to be merged with enough hydrogen nuclei to grow gigantic before he got a chance to merge."

"Hydrogen nuclei?"

"Yes. The same technique was used by the Human Lord Rutherford, just after the turn of the twentieth century. He used high-level radiation to transmute nitrogen into oxygen."

Julie thought about that for a moment. "So I guess chemistry really did replace alchemy."

"Yes," Tungsten agreed, "but it grew out of it as well."

Julie nodded. Then a thought occurred to her. "Tungsten, why would Wendelium lie about his origins?"

"Perhaps he wanted to keep them a secret."

"But why? What did he have to gain?"

Tungsten considered the question before answering. "Perhaps he wanted to study the phenomenon."

Julie sighed. "He wanted to be a real element. Desperately so. He doesn't have any element in the Human world to supervise, any chores to do, any duties to fulfill. So what's he up to?"

Julie and Tungsten exchanged nervous looks. Still concerned, Julie opened her desk drawer to retrieve a pencil, in order to mark off on her calendar that Tungsten had shown up. But as she put her hand into the drawer, she felt something made of hard, cool metal.

Surprised, she brought out the object. It was a small, dark gray box, exactly like the one Lithium had given her on her first journey to Mathematics, complete with a similar figure of a running horse. However, instead of "Li," another chemical symbol was engraved across the top: "Wd."

"Tungsten," she said, "I think I know what Wendelium has been up to. He's created duties for himself."

"What do you mean?"

Julie held up the box. "His element exists in the Human world now."

A Brief Glossary of Scientific Terms

alchemy: A very old set of beliefs that helped create chemistry, because many people experimented with elements so they could make gold or live forever or reach perfection, etc. Their experiments did not make them reach their various goals, but they did cause a lot of scientific materials and methods to be discovered.

atom: An invisibly small bit of matter that has negative-charged parts (electrons), positive-charged parts (protons), and electrically neutral parts (neutrons). Everything in the universe is made up of some kind of atom or another. Atoms are named according to how many protons they have — that is, which element they are.

electron: A negative-charged part of an atom that spins wildly around the atom's central part in an orbit that has a specific shape. This orbit is called a "shell" because it is three-dimensional, not just a circle. The shape of each electron's shell is defined by how many electrons the atom has and which number that specific electron has (they are all numbered starting at 1). For example, if a given electron is number four, its shell would be shaped like a figure eight.

element: A collection of atoms that have the same number of protons; for instance, all atoms with six protons are called carbon.

ion: An atom that has lost or gained one or more electrons.

isotope: A specific kind of element, defined by the number of neutrons it has. For instance, all carbon has six protons, but carbon atoms with six neutrons are called carbon-12 (because they add the protons and neutrons), and carbon atoms with eight neutrons are called carbon-14.

lepton: A theoretical bit of an atom that is even smaller than electrons and protons. Electrons are made of these.

neutron: A tiny bit of an atom which has no electrical charge. Different numbers of neutrons define the different isotopes of an element.

Periodic Table: A chart invented by Dmitri Mendeleev (1834–1907) that organizes all the known elements into rows and columns according to the number of protons plus neutrons (atomic mass) they have.

proton: A positive-charged part of an atom that is found in the central part of the atom, which is called the nucleus. The number of protons an atom has defines which element it is.

About the Author

Wendy Isdell began writing her first book, *A Gebra Named Al*, when she was in the eighth grade. She entered the story in the Virginia Young Author's Contest of 1989, where it won first place in the Rappahannock regional competition and went on to capture first place at the state level. She sent her story to Free Spirit Publishing in 1992, and it was published in 1993, when Wendy was a senior in high school.

She began writing *The Chemy Called Al* three months before *A Gebra Named Al* was accepted for publication. She set *Chemy* aside to finish *Gebra* and her high school studies, and completed the last three-fourths of it over winter break of 1993–1994.

Wendy is currently studying for her bachelor's degree at a private university, where she enjoys playing her guitar, hanging out with friends, talking to her plants, and producing her own television shows for the university station. Her eventual goal is to make enough of a living from her writing to support herself.

Also available from Free Spirit Publishing

Using The Chemy Called Al in the Classroom
by Wendy Isdell. Includes questions, problems, and
activities that bring the novel into the curriculum.
Softcover, 32 pp., 8 ½" x 11". Grades 7 & up. $6.95

A Gebra Named Al: *A Novel by
Wendy Isdell.* Julie hates algebra —
until she meets a gebra named Al.
Julie, Al, and the Periodic horses
journey through the Land of Mathematics, where
the Orders of Operations are real places and fruits
like Bohr models grow on chemistrees. Wonderfully
written and a joy to read, it's full of math and science basics made fun.
Softcover, 128 pp., 5 ⅛" x 7 ½". Ages 11 & up. $4.95.

Using A Gebra Named Al in the Classroom
by Wendy Isdell. Includes questions, problems, and
activities that bring the novel into the curriculum.
Softcover, 32 pp., 8 ½" x 11". Grades 6 & up. $6.95.

Find these books in your favorite bookstore, or write or call:

Free Spirit Publishing Inc.
400 First Avenue North, Suite 616
Minneapolis, MN 55401-1730
Toll-free (800) 735-7323, Local (612) 338-2068
Fax (612) 337-5050
E-mail help4kids@freespirit.com